To Mark Gatiss, a great fan of the Baker Street boy, who helps to
keep the Sherlockian flame burning brightly.

the further adventures of

SHERLOCK HOLMES

THE RIPPER LEGACY

THE RIPPER LEGACY

DAVID STUART DAVIES

TITAN BOOKS

THE FURTHER ADVENTURES OF SHERLOCK HOLMES:
THE RIPPER LEGACY
Print edition ISBN: 9781783296590
E-book edition ISBN: 9781783296606

Published by Titan Books
A division of Titan Publishing Group Ltd
144 Southwark Street, London SE1 0UP

First edition: July 2016
10 9 8 7 6 5 4 3 2 1

A CIP catalogue record for this title is available from the British Library.

Printed in the USA.

Dr Watson's Journal

I was not blessed with children. It was one of the great sadnesses of my life, but Fate decreed that I should never become a parent. When I married my beloved Mary, we both thought that in time we would have a baby. Ideally I wanted a boy and a girl. The girl would possess all the qualities of my intelligent and beautiful wife, and the boy would carry on the name of Watson with what I hoped would be distinction and honour. But it was not to be.

Both Mary and I were of the mind that the first few years of our married life should be devoted to one another. We thought that there would be plenty of time to introduce little strangers into our domestic situation later on. But in the fourth year of our marriage, Mary fell victim to a series of illnesses that in themselves were not life threatening but in combination seriously weakened her constitution. When she caught diphtheria in that cursed winter of 1892, she had little reserve to fight it. She was brave to the end, but nothing that I or my colleagues administered could prevent her from succumbing. Towards the end, I saw her gradually fading before my eyes, slowly evolving into a ghost.

Mary died in my arms.

I not only lost my wife that terrible day but so many of my dreams and, if I'm truthful, I do believe that I was never quite the same man again.

When Mary died I was already suffering a loss – one, however, that proved not to be permanent. My friend, Sherlock Holmes, the best and wisest man I knew, had disappeared from my life in 1891. I believed that he had tumbled into the roaring torrent of the Reichenbach Falls, in a death tussle with Professor James Moriarty. As I learned later, this was not the case. Moriarty had perished, but Holmes had escaped the same watery fate and effectively absented himself from public life for the next three years. I knew nothing of his remarkable escape and when he eventually returned to London after a time travelling on the continent and beyond, and walked back into my lonely life, I was so overjoyed to see him that any resentment that may have flamed in my breast at his deception was doused in the joy of the reunion.

Within a short time of his reappearance I had returned to our rooms in Baker Street and resumed my station in the armchair by the fire opposite my friend. 'It is quite like the old days,' he observed, one evening shortly after my reinstatement, as he idly plucked the strings of his violin.

I nodded and gave him a brief smile. But, in truth, it was not like the old days. We were both slightly damaged, different men from those two young fellows who first began sharing rooms together many years ago. Life certainly had taken its toll on me. I had loved and lost. There would always be an empty dark corner in my life now. In those idle moments that come upon one unexpectedly, I found my mind going back to my days with Mary: our courtship, our marriage, and those quiet evenings together. All gone.

Often I would see a lady in the street with her children and felt a physical pain of regret and longing. Of course, I would never reveal these feelings to Sherlock Holmes. He had little time for emotion and the world of domestic happiness was alien to him and held no interest for his clinical and oh so rational mind.

These were my secret thoughts and feelings, as I'm sure Holmes had his own, and we guarded them cautiously lest we reveal any inkling of their content. My friend, too, had suffered the slings and arrows of capricious fortune and his brush with death had brought intimations of his own mortality into his purview. He was still the enigmatic fellow I had first encountered, the brilliant thinker and detective, but somehow he was also a sadder man. Like the old days? In so many ways, yes. On the surface at least. But in other ways, no. Life had bruised us.

I have long resisted recounting the dark and dramatic details of the Temple kidnapping case for many reasons; some of them political, but mainly because it involved the loss of a child, something that had such a strong effect upon me emotionally. I have to confess I am not sure I know why I have decided to do so now, unless it is to ease the disquiet I feel when I recall this investigation and that the act of putting the details down on paper will be some kind of catharsis. Who can say?

It was a very wet day in the March of 1895. A net of rain held the capital in its thrall. As evening approached the leaden skies gave no hope of relief. I had returned to Baker Street after spending a desultory afternoon at my club. I had intended to have a game of billiards with my usual partner, Thurston, but he was not around so, after taking a light lunch, I mooched in the reading room perusing the papers, allowing boredom to take hold. I would have walked home had it not been for the rain, so instead resorted to the comfort and convenience of a cab.

As I entered our sitting room, shaking off my wet coat, I saw that Holmes had a visitor, a dark-suited young man, who sat opposite my friend in my armchair. He was leaning forward almost in a pose of supplication and, to my surprise, he seemed to be crying. His eyes were moist and his cheeks were damp. As I moved further into the room, he turned his face from me.

'Ah,' said Holmes briskly. 'Here is my friend and associate, Dr Watson. Returned early from his club without the pleasure of his usual game of billiards, I see.'

'How did...' I stopped and gave a wry grin. I was used to this kind of recital by now, but that did not prevent me from being surprised by the accuracy of Holmes's deduction.

'No billiard chalk in your sleeve as there usually is and no pencil marks on your cuff where you make your calculations,' Holmes responded, answering my half-formed question, before throwing a languid arm in the direction of our visitor. 'Let me introduce you to Mr Ronald Temple, who has brought a little puzzle to our door for us to solve.' Apparently unperturbed by the young man's distress, Holmes turned to him with a cold smile. 'Dr Watson is an invaluable aid to my detective work. I would like him to hear your story also. I trust that is agreeable?'

Ronald Temple did not seem capable of a verbal response and just nodded his head. Holmes glanced at me, his expression revealing that he realised perhaps he had been too brusque and businesslike in his treatment of our potential client. 'I think perhaps Mr Temple could do with a brandy to steel him for the task of repeating his sad tale. If you would be so kind, Watson...'

Without a word I poured Mr Temple a brandy and slipped the glass between his nervous fingers. I was struck by how pale and cold they were. Indeed, the fellow was so inanimate and unresponsive that he appeared to be in some kind of trance. He was a tall, good-looking fellow, somewhere in his mid-thirties, with strong, intelligent features. His neat blonde hair was anointed with pomade, which shone in the firelight rather like some artificial halo. His clothes, although somewhat crumpled, were well cut and expensive. Dark circles beneath his eyes bore witness to several sleepless nights. Whatever problem he had brought to the door of Sherlock Holmes, his features reflected the anguish that it caused.

'Do take a drink,' said Holmes. 'It will help to fortify you.'

Like a child, Mr Temple did as he was told. I pulled up a chair and waited.

'Now,' said Holmes, more gently, 'if you'll begin again, Mr Temple.'

We waited a few moments for our visitor to respond to Holmes's request. He seemed distracted and weighed down with a disabling soulful burden, but at length he spoke. The words emerged as a hoarse whisper, flat and unemotional, belying the tortured expression on his face.

'He's been taken. William. He's been kidnapped. Stolen from us.'

'And William is...' prompted my friend gently.

'My son. William. He is eight years of age. He has been kidnapped. Taken.'

'The police know of this?' I asked gently, my heart going out to the distressed fellow.

He nodded and for the first time turned to me as though he

had just become aware of my presence. 'They have found nothing. They are lost. Just as we are.'

Holmes leaned forward and addressed Temple in a quiet, soothing manner.

'Please, Mr Temple, give us the relevant facts and pray be precise as to detail. We need to know your whole story before we can assess the situation.'

Temple took a sip of brandy and began.

'I am a stockbroker in the city and even if I say so myself, I am very successful in my profession. As a result I live a very comfortable life with a pleasant house in Cricklewood. I am married to my childhood sweetheart, Charlotte, and we have the happiest of marriages. Our happiness was increased when eight years ago our son William was born. He is a bright, intelligent fellow and...' Temple paused, his voice cracking, and he gazed down unseeingly into the brandy glass.

Holmes and I remained silent and waited for him to regain his composure, which he did after another sip of brandy.

'Six days ago, he travelled up to town with my wife and his nanny, Mrs Susan Gordon, a widowed lady who has been in her post since William was a baby. They visited the Natural History Museum – William is currently fascinated by dinosaurs – and then went for a stroll in Kensington Gardens. They walked by the lake, William rushing ahead as young boys do. For a brief moment Charlotte and Mrs Gordon lost sight of him in the crowd. At first they weren't concerned. William is a good lad and they knew he would come back to them in time. And then... and then...' Temple shook his head as though in denial, not wanting to reveal the next part of his narrative. 'And then, they saw William in the company of two men, each holding him firmly by the hands, virtually dragging him away from the lake towards the entrance of the park. William seemed distressed and appeared to be struggling to be free of their hold, but to no avail. The brutes had him firmly in their grasp. My wife and Mrs Gordon were momentarily frozen with shock and horror at what they saw and then when the full realisation of what was happening dawned on them, they gave chase. They were hindered in their pursuit by the crowds and at one point a woman with a perambulator crashed into Charlotte, knocking her down. When they were able to resume their chase, William and the two men had… disappeared. Gone. There was no sign of them anywhere. The poor boy had been snatched from us.'

With these words he slumped back in his chair, the strain of recounting this haunting incident etched deep in his pale features.

'What happened next?' prompted Holmes after a pause.

'We contacted the police and a search was instigated, but nothing was found. They seem at a loss at what to do other than wait to see if the boy turns up. That is hardly likely.'

'Has there been a ransom note?' I asked.

Temple shook his head. 'We've heard nothing.'

Holmes steepled his fingers and gazed directly at Temple. 'Can you think of any reason why your son was taken?'

'None. He's just an ordinary little boy. I am comfortably off but I am not rich.'

'What about the two men who abducted William? Could your wife describe them?'

'Only in the vaguest terms. She never really saw their faces – just from the side. They were tall, muscular men, probably middle-aged, and dressed in dark clothing. We are in a deep, dark fog, Mr

Holmes. I come to you in desperation. Can you find our boy? Can you return him to us?'

Holmes's features, lit by the firelight, looked grim as he replied. 'I do not know. It would be wrong of me to give you false hope. There is very little to grasp in this case. Strangers snatch your son and disappear. There seems to be no motive other than the possession of a young boy.'

'Then we are lost. Lost.' Temple ran his fingers across his brow in a distracted fashion, his eyes moistening with tears once more.

'Not quite, I hope. Indeed, hope is all I can offer you at present,' said Holmes. 'But beware, for it is only a slender hope. I just need the thinnest of threads so I can begin to ravel it slowly towards a solution. But there has to be that thread. I will look into the matter and see what I can do.'

This news brightened the face of our visitor and his features briefly fashioned themselves into a ghost of a smile. 'Bless you, sir. Bless you.'

'Please remember I can promise no miracles. One cannot make bricks without clay. It is essential I gain as much information about the kidnapping as possible. Therefore the first thing we should do is accompany you to your home so that I can talk with your wife and the nanny, Mrs Gordon. As they were major players in this drama, what they have to say may be of great use.'

Our journey to Cricklewood by hansom cab was carried out in silence, each of us lost in our own thoughts. No doubt Holmes was weighing up the meagre facts in his mind and contemplating the various scenarios that could result from them. His brows were contracted and those steely eyes had a faraway look, but it was the thin lips compressed and turned down that told me of his deep unease. By contrast Temple's face was a blank. He was obviously exhausted and the strain of his situation had drained him of all emotion and thought for the moment.

Cedar Lodge was a smart Georgian villa set in its own grounds, approached by a curving tree-lined drive. The door was opened to us by a tall stately woman with strong aquiline features, emphasised by the fact that her straw-coloured hair was pulled back in a severe bun. She greeted Temple with a chaste kiss on the cheek.

'This is my sister-in-law, Hilda Bennett. Mr Holmes and Dr Watson.'

We shook hands and exchanged muted pleasantries.

'Charlotte is resting. I'll let her know that you have returned,' Miss Bennett said.

Temple nodded. 'Please do. Mr Holmes would like to have words with her.'

With a brief nod, and a rustle of her skirt, she disappeared into the recesses of the house.

We were taken into a large, pleasant drawing room with French windows, which gave a view of a lawn and shrubbery beyond. A fire crackled and flickered in the hearth.

'Please make yourself at home, gentlemen. I will arrange for some tea,' said our host.

Without another word he left us. This was the first occasion that Holmes and I had been alone together since we had heard Temple's sad story.

'Well, Holmes,' I said quietly, 'what do you make of it?'

He shook his head sadly. 'It is hopeless, Watson. Absolutely hopeless.'

Two

'Poor mite. He ain't eating still. He'll waste away if he goes on much longer like this.'

The woman wiped her nose with the back of her hand and threw the plate into the sink. The sound of it echoed around the shabby chamber.

'Hey, you silly cow,' cried her husband with fervour, 'I could've ate that.'

'Ah, it's gone cold now.'

'Still…' He pursed his lips and, with a petulant gesture, pulled a wooden chair away from the table nearer the fire. 'The young gentleman'll learn in time. Two or three more days and he'll be ready to eat a dead rat. You mark my words.'

The woman gave a wheezy laugh. 'I'd like to see you serve that up to him.'

The man grinned. 'Rats is rich in vittles.' He chuckled wheezily.

'You are a devil, Percy. You really are.' The woman smiled, revealing a mouth that had lost most of its teeth.

'Well, maybe. I'd certainly prefer to be about some devilish business rather than turning into a nursery maid.'

'It won't be for much longer. At least that's what he said.'

'Aye, maybe.' Absentmindedly, he examined his fingers; large, fleshy, dirt-ingrained appendages atop a huge hand. He clenched them into a fist and punched the air. 'I miss the ring,' he muttered to himself.

'Ah, you're too old and slow for that game now.'

He gave a grunt of annoyance. He knew that she was right and this made the knowledge all the more painful. He rubbed the gnarled growth on the side of his head which a thousand punches ago had been an ear. 'I need some ale.' He rose from the chair and made for the door.

'You don't be late and don't come back roarin' drunk. We have responsibilities, Percy, which we're paid handsomely for.'

'Yes, yes,' he said, grabbing his overcoat from the coat hook. 'I'll be a good boy.' He gurgled mirthfully and left.

The woman, Annie Grimes, sat for some time by the fire gazing at the flames, her mind free of thought, and then with a sigh she rose with some purpose. Candlestick in hand she made her way up the rickety staircase to the first room on the landing. She unlocked the door and peered inside. The boy lay curled on the rough sacking that served as his bed. He appeared to be asleep.

'Hungry yet?' said Annie, not unkindly.

There was no response.

Her expression soured. 'Please yourself then,' she said, closing and locking the door.

Three

Dr Watson's Journal

Charlotte Temple was a very pretty woman in her early thirties. She was shorter and rounder than her sister and her features were somehow softer and kinder. It was clear that she had applied some extra face powder to hide the dark circles under her eyes and the ravages of sleepless nights that had marred her beauty. She shook both our hands gently, appearing somewhat wary of us, and then joined her husband on the sofa. Her sister, Hilda, sat upright in a chair by the drawing-room window.

'I know how very trying this must be for you,' said Holmes sympathetically, 'but I do not ask you to recount the events of the day your son disappeared lightly. It may be that one trifling piece of information that you are able to give me may be of vital importance. We shall have to see.' When he wanted to – usually in the pursuit of evidence for a case – Holmes could be remarkably gentle and persuasive with the opposite sex. It was a talent rather than a natural facility.

Charlotte Temple shifted her position on the sofa as though she was nervous, but she replied in a clear, forthright manner: 'I am more than happy to go over the events again if they have only an infinitesimal chance of providing a clue to where my little boy is.'

'Good,' said Holmes with a smile. 'So, this excursion to London. Had it been planned for a while?'

'It was a belated birthday treat. William had a heavy cold on his birthday so the celebrations were somewhat muted. I promised him this trip when he was feeling better. We travelled up to town in the morning...'

'We?'

'William, my husband and Mrs Gordon, our nanny. My husband went off to his work and we visited the Natural History Museum. It was a very happy occasion.'

'Were you conscious of anyone following you or did you perhaps see certain individuals more than once in different locations?'

Charlotte Temple shook her head. 'No. Nothing like that,' she said without hesitation.

'Did anything unusual happen at all while you were at the museum?'

'No, not that I can recall...'

'Anything?'

Mrs Temple thought hard for some moments before replying. 'Well, I was almost pushed to the ground by a fellow desperate to leave the building. He collided with me as he rushed past in a terrible hurry, knocking me sideways, and for a moment I feared I might lose my balance. He muttered his apologies without stopping.'

'Could you describe him?'

She closed her eyes as though trying to bring an image of this man to mind. 'It all happened so fast and I thought nothing of it.

He was youngish, dark-haired and tall. Oh, and he carried a silver-headed cane.'

Holmes nodded. 'Thank you. What happened after you visited the museum?'

'We walked to Kensington Gardens. Our plan was to stroll about a little in the sunshine, watch the model boats on the Round Pond and then take William for a late lunch at a restaurant near to where my husband works. He was due to join us there.'

'The two men you saw who took William away – did you observe them before the abduction? Loitering nearby, perhaps?'

'Oh, Mr Holmes, this is a question that haunts me. I cannot be sure. Sometimes my mind says that I did. At other times, I think I'm fooling myself.'

'I understand. Now please describe to me in precise detail what happened when William was taken.'

Charlotte Temple clasped her husband's hand and took a deep breath before responding. 'William had become fascinated by one of the boats on the pond, a little white-masted schooner. He rushed along the edge of the water keeping up with its progress. As a result, his enthusiasm caused him to run well ahead of Mrs Gordon and me and then... and then...' She faltered momentarily, but resumed her narrative with added steel in her voice. 'He disappeared from our sight, lost in the throng at the edge of the pond. At first we were not in any way alarmed, but as we quickened our pace to catch up with him we realised we could not see him – had no idea where he was. There were crowds that day and it was so easy to get lost in the crush. We began calling his name. And then, as we broke through a knot of people, we saw in the distance two men taking William away with them. They were virtually dragging him along at great speed.'

'What were these men like?'

'Again I can only give you the sketchiest of details. They were tall, brutish, I should say. Not gentlemen. That's about all, I'm afraid.'

'What happened next?'

'We hastened after these men, calling out, but we were hindered by the crowd who took no notice of our cries and then out of nowhere it seemed this woman ran into us with a pram and winded me. I fell to the ground briefly.'

'This woman – what was she like?'

'Well, I assume she wasn't the mother of the baby for she appeared quite advanced in years. A rough-looking woman, rather shabbily dressed. I certainly wouldn't have wanted her to be in charge of any child of mine.'

'Did you see the baby?'

Charlotte Temple seemed surprised at this question and her brow furrowed. 'Well... no not really. The hood of the pram was up... but she'd hardly be pushing an empty perambulator would she?'

Holmes pursed his lips. 'Quite.'

'What did this woman say? Did she apologise?' I asked.

'No, she did not. She told me to mind where I was going and to get out of her way.'

'A charming soul.'

'I took little notice of her ill manners. I was desperate to catch up with the two men who had my boy, but by the time we resumed our chase they had... disappeared.'

Mrs Temple gave a sharp intake of breath and lowered her head as though the retelling of these dreadful details had robbed her of all energy. My heart went out to this poor distressed soul.

'Why would they take him, Mr Holmes, for what reason?' This question came from Hilda Bennett.

'There are several possible reasons, but it would be futile to discuss them in detail now until we have more data. However, it does seem that a ransom is not one of them. There has been no communication from the kidnappers?'

Mrs Temple shook her head.

'Do you have a photograph of your son? It will help greatly in our investigation.'

Mrs Temple nodded assent. 'I will select one for you. Perhaps you also ought to know that William has a birthmark. On his shoulder.' She indicated the location on her own body. 'It is in the shape of a triangle or pyramid. It is very distinctive.'

Holmes jotted this down in his notebook. 'Excellent. That is most useful to know. And now perhaps I could have words with Mrs Gordon.'

'She can only tell you what my wife has done,' said Temple. There was a brittleness in his voice, borne no doubt of frustration and tiredness.

'Nevertheless...' responded Holmes gently.

Mrs Susan Gordon was a homely soul, a lady in her early sixties I should guess, and one who radiated both warmth and reliability. We interviewed her alone in her private sitting room and indeed she gave the very same account of the abduction as Mrs Temple, but Holmes questioned her further.

'These wonderful samples of needlepoint I see around me are your work, I suspect,' he said with some enthusiasm.

The lady smiled. 'Yes, they are.'

'They are exquisite. You have a keen eye to perform work in such detail.'

'I believe so,' she replied modestly.

'I am now going to call upon those eyes to describe to me the two men you saw take young Master William.'

'Oh, it all happened so quickly... there really wasn't time to notice much.'

'Not much, but something.'

She hesitated for a moment, her brow furrowing gently. 'Well, yes, I suppose it's possible.'

'Take your mind back to the incident. Form an image in your mind. Think hard. You are back in Kensington Gardens. There are people all around you. Young William – you see him ahead of you, by the water's edge...'

'Yes... yes I do,' Mrs Gordon replied breathily, her body erect and her gaze directed into the far distance.

'Now,' said Holmes, leaning towards the woman, 'you see the two men, tall...'

'One was taller than the other. The shorter one was stout and had wispy hair sticking out beneath his cap.'

'A cap, not a hat.'

'Yes, a cap: one of those large tweed things – like the raised crust on a mutton pie.'

'Good. What else? What about his features?'

'I only saw him sideways, in profile. There wasn't a lot to see.'

'Clean-shaven?'

Mrs Gordon hesitated a moment. 'Why no. He had a moustache, a big one. The sort that hangs over the lip. What do you call them?'

'A walrus moustache.'

'That's it.'

'What age was this man would you say?'

'Difficult to say. The hair was greyish. Probably in his forties, maybe late forties.'

'And what of his clothes?'

Mrs Gordon thought a while then smiled. 'Why, now you come to mention it, I believe he was wearing checked trousers.'

Holmes threw me a satisfied glance. 'And what about the other fellow? The tall one.'

'Oh, he was an ugly brute. His features were large. Great big bulbous nose and pockmarked skin. And one of his ears, well it was like some sort of gnarled growth on the side of his head.' She shuddered at the thought.

'Excellent.' Holmes clapped his hands with pleasure.

Mrs Gordon smiled benignly. 'I had no idea that I remembered so much.'

'The mind takes in many things subconsciously; it's just that we need to take extra coaxing to retrieve them. You have done most excellently.'

'Will it help?'

'I hope so. I truly hope so.'

Some ten minutes later we took our leave of Mr and Mrs Temple. Holmes had secured a photograph of the missing boy and assured them he would do his best to discover the whereabouts of their son.

On the cab ride back to Baker Street Holmes said little. He sat, his shoulders hunched inside his ulster with his chin resting on his chest like some great brooding bird. I knew that in moments like this there was little point in trying to engage my friend in conversation. I was aware that he was deep in thought about the case, removed mentally from his physical surroundings, and I had no intention of interrupting his musings.

It wasn't until late that evening, when we sat by our fireside sipping a nightcap, that I referred to the desperate business that he had been summoned to resolve.

'Have you developed any theories regarding the matter?' I asked in as casual a manner as I could muster.

Holmes gave a derisive snort. 'I am a detective, not a magician. I cannot conjure up a solution out of thin air. I need data, facts, evidence. Only then can I function with some efficacy.'

'Was there nothing you learned today that is of any use?'

Holmes pursed his lips. 'A little. The two abductors are no doubt of the fancy sporting types. The tweed cap and checked trousers are *de rigueur* for the track and the ring and the brutish fellow with the bulbous nose and cauliflower ear is most likely a boxer, probably an ex-boxer now that he is employed in such nefarious activities as kidnapping. And I use the word 'employed' carefully, for it is clear to me that these two fellows are hired hands. Individuals of that ilk are not the progenitors of such crimes as kidnapping, they are merely worker bees. There is something dark and dangerous about this business, I am convinced of it. It goes much deeper than a simple kidnapping. It troubles me greatly.' He stared into the dying flames and sighed.

I came down to breakfast the following morning quite early, but Holmes was already up and I found him at the table examining the photograph of young William Temple that his mother had given to us. As I sat by my friend, he passed it to me. 'Do you notice anything odd about this photograph?' he asked.

I had looked at it the day before and seen nothing that could be regarded as odd. It had obviously been taken in a photographer's studio and featured a young boy, sitting on a small bench staring easily at the camera. He seemed a gentle soul with dark curly hair and wide innocent eyes. I studied it for some moments, but I could not see anything that might have aroused Holmes's interest. I passed the photograph back to him with a shake of the head.

'You're going to have to tell me,' I said, reaching over for the coffee pot.

'What if I give you a clue?' His eyes twinkled mischievously.

'Bit early in the morning to be sitting an exam,' I grinned. 'Oh, very well. Give me a clue.'

'The hair and the nose,' he said, holding the photograph up for me.

I looked again.

'I see nothing of consequence,' I said.

'Cast your mind back to yesterday and the faces of the parents: to their narrow clean-cut features. Both mother and father have fine aquiline noses and prominent chins and light, straight, almost straw-coloured hair. Now look at the boy: round features, broad fleshy nose, dark curly hair and wide eyes. In the great scheme of life the offspring resembles at least one of the parents...'

'What on earth are you saying...?' Of course, I knew what my friend was implying, but I needed him to confirm it in words.

'The boy is not their natural son.'

I looked again at the photograph. I could see what Holmes meant by the complete lack of similarity between the boy and his parents. It hadn't occurred to me, but now Holmes had pointed it out it seemed obvious.

'What on earth does this mean?' I asked.

'Well, it means that we haven't been told the whole truth, the full story. There is more to this matter than has been revealed to us.'

I shook my head in disbelief. 'Why would they do that?'

'That is something I intend to find out.' He rose and pushed back his chair. 'Drink up, Watson. We leave for Cedar Lodge in five minutes.'

Four

'I believe that you are refusing to eat, young sir,' said the tall man with the large shiny hat and the silver-topped cane, as he leant casually against the doorjamb.

'I want to go home. I want to see my parents,' said the boy. There was no fear in the voice, but the man could tell he was close to tears.

'I am afraid that is not going to be possible. Not for the moment at least. But you must keep up your strength if you want to see them again. I'm sure your mother would not wish you to starve.'

'Let me go.'

'You see, sir, the little blighter won't be told,' observed Annie Grimes, who materialised behind the tall gentleman.

'The pangs of hunger are a mighty persuader, Mrs Grimes. When he is near death's door, we may have to force-feed him. You wouldn't like that, would you, boy? Think on it.' He grinned and Annie Grimes cackled.

Slowly, the man closed the door, plunging the boy into the grey gloom of the windowless chamber. He gazed disconsolately at the plate of cold mince on the table. Tempting though it was despite its ugly, congealed appearance, William determined that he would not give in. As if to prove it, more to himself than to his captors, he picked the plate up and threw it face down on the floor.

The tall man with the silver-topped cane placed two sovereigns in Annie Grimes' claw-like hand. 'It won't be long now before we take the boy away. I am just awaiting the word from my master,' he said silkily.

Mrs Grimes hardly heard these words as she gazed admiringly at the two gold coins. 'Whatever you say, sir,' she said absentmindedly, slipping the sovereigns into her apron pocket.

Five

Dr Watson's Journal

Charlotte Temple seemed very surprised to see us so soon after our last visit. 'You have news,' she cried excitedly, running towards my friend as we entered the drawing room.

Holmes shook his head. 'Alas, no. It is too soon to hope for developments, but I believe that you have information for *me*.'

Mrs Temple's eyebrows rose in surprise. 'I am afraid that I do not understand you, Mr Holmes.'

My friend sighed. 'I do not wish to be indelicate, but you have not confided in us the absolute truth. By omission you have concealed an important piece of evidence. The boy William is not your natural son, is he?'

Charlotte Temple paled and dropped down on to the sofa. For some moments she seemed lost for words.

'I don't know what you mean,' she said at last.

'I think you do. I would not raise this point if it were not of the utmost importance in this case. I think it would be wise if you told us the truth.'

'The truth? Oh, the truth.' She took a lace handkerchief from her sleeve and dabbed her eyes, which had begun to water. 'The truth isn't something we have thought about or talked about for years.'

'Well, perhaps it is time to do so now. It may save the life of your son.'

Mrs Temple's eyes widened. 'What do you mean?'

'I would rather not discuss half-formed theories at present. Not until I have all the facts of the matter to hand. So, if you would be so kind...'

She pursed her lips and gave a sigh of resignation. 'Very well. You are right. William is not our true son. I cannot have children. We found that out to our great regret nearly ten years ago. It was a tremendous blow to both my husband and me and nearly destroyed our marriage. It was a desperate time for us. And then Ronald learned of an establishment... somewhere we could adopt a child.'

'A baby farm,' said Holmes, making no attempt to keep the note of distaste from his voice.

Mrs Temple nodded. 'A baby farm. I know what you must be thinking. I am aware that these places are regarded as being... disreputable.'

'To say the least,' snapped Holmes.

My friend was correct. Baby farms were establishments where unwanted and illegitimate children were taken in for a payment. These places often ill-treated the infants or even murdered them once the money was paid. Some offered the children up for adoption to those unfortunate couples who could not have children of their own, but the whole trade was shabby and illegal.

'When one is desperate, Mr Holmes, one grasps at straws. And we were desperate for a child and here was an opportunity to make our family complete.'

'It is not my position to judge you in this matter, madam.'

Her eyes flashed with anger and her body stiffened. 'You certainly are not, sir. Your implied censure is misplaced. You cannot appreciate the despair one feels at being unable to have a child when you ache to have one. It colours your whole life. We felt our household incomplete without a little one to care for. And when an opportunity presents itself to help you achieve this ambition, however circuitous and unconventional, all you do is thank your good fortune. In reality, we rescued a young boy from a terrible fate and gave him a good home filled with affection and care. Who knows if he would have survived without our help? In our eyes, William is our true son; the bond and love between us is as strong and secure as if we were his natural parents.'

Charlotte Temple spoke with such passion that my friend seemed somewhat taken aback. He bowed his head. 'I am sorry for appearing insensitive to your plight. As Dr Watson will avow there are some occasions when I fail to respond appropriately to a situation. I understand and appreciate all that you have told me. Please forgive me.'

Mrs Temple gave a brief nod of acknowledgement.

'Does William know that he is adopted?' Holmes asked after a brief pause.

'No. I am afraid both my husband and I shied away from the prospect of telling him. In truth we were torn between the desire to let him know the truth and maintaining the myth that he really was truly and fully ours.'

'I will need details of this establishment, this baby farm.'

'Good heavens! Why?'

'It is where the trail begins and it may lead us to where the trail ends. This is not an idle request, I assure you.'

For a moment, Mrs Temple did not respond and then she rose from the sofa in a swift movement. 'Very well, if you think it is important.'

'I do.'

'Please wait here.' Without another word she left the room, leaving us alone.

Holmes turned to me and placed a finger to his lips. 'Not a word of censure, Watson. I know I was a little… crass. I have made amends.'

I said nothing, but rolled my eyes in a disapproving fashion.

In a few moments, Mrs Temple returned with a sheet of paper, which she handed to Holmes. 'This is the address of the establishment. The woman in charge was a Mrs Chandler. Gertrude Chandler. But of course that was eight years ago.'

'Thank you,' said Holmes, folding the paper and placing it in his pocket. 'Come, Watson, our business here is done. We have work to do. I shall be in touch in due course, Mrs Temple, when I hope we shall have news for you.'

Dr Watson's Journal

On returning to our cab, Holmes gave the driver an address in Camberwell. I assumed that it was the address of the baby farm.

'What do you think you will learn there?' I asked as we rattled along.

'Well, the obvious,' replied Holmes smugly.

'Which is?'

'The name of the boy's true parents or more likely just that of his mother, for it's likely that the boy was born out of wedlock and the mother was abandoned once the father had found she was with child. That is the common scenario.'

It was a sad but realistic assessment. While I had not encountered such cases in my own rather staid medical practice, I had heard of many such from colleagues working at St Bart's and St Thomas' Hospital: women cast aside by their men once in the family way, as to brutes of a certain mentality a child was an unnecessary financial encumbrance. This placed the mother in a terrible dilemma.

Some sought to end the pregnancy by medical intervention; some brave souls attempted to bring the child up themselves and resorted to prostitution to secure the means of doing so; and some, in dark desperation, murdered the child once it had been born. And then there were those who passed their baby on to the kind of establishment we were about to visit. These thoughts passed through my mind as we made our way to Camberwell and cast a shadow over my mood.

We travelled south of the river and eventually the cab pulled up outside a detached property on John Ruskin Street off the Walworth Road. It was a large undistinguished house and it had seen better days. It stood a little back from the road and the small garden that fronted it was mere scrubland, dotted with sickly plants. Paint was peeling from the door and window frames. The whole place had a forlorn and neglected air about it.

Holmes instructed the cabbie to wait for us once more and we made our way up the path and used the rusty knocker to announce our presence. Some moments later the door was opened by a scrap of a girl dressed in a shabby housemaid's uniform. She curtsied in a clumsy mechanical fashion.

'How can I help you gents?' she asked.

Holmes smiled in an uncharacteristically ingratiating fashion. 'We have business with Mrs Chandler. Be so good as to inform her of our arrival.' So saying he took a step forward over the threshold, causing the girl to retreat into the hallway. Suitably intimidated by Holmes's forthright nature and imposing presence, she curtsied again and with a nervous frown scurried off down the hall into the gloom beyond.

Holmes gave a little chuckle. 'She's only little more than a baby herself,' he murmured.

After a short wait, a tall, thin woman appeared before us. She had gaunt, angular features and the most penetrating blue eyes I have seen. Her hair was swept back into a tight bun that emphasised the severity of her expression. I would have placed her in her mid-forties, but she could have been older. She was dressed in a long amber silk dress, more suitable, I would have thought, for an evening soirée than the daytime.

'I am Mrs Chandler. Is it business, gentlemen?' she asked. Her tone was cool and formal although not unpleasant, but there was no warmth in those eyes.

'Yes,' said Holmes.

'Then you'd better come into my office.' Without another word, she turned and with a swish of her dress retraced her steps, leading us down the hall to a door.

'Come in, gentlemen,' she said, holding it open for us.

The chamber was small and cluttered. There was a desk, a small table harbouring an empty decanter and some glasses, several chairs and an enormous aspidistra in the corner. She bade us take a seat while she positioned herself behind the desk, which was strewn with papers.

'You have a child?' she said, leaning back in her chair.

'We do not,' said Holmes sharply.

She raised her eyebrows in mild surprise. 'You want a child?'

Holmes shook his head. 'We come on a different kind of business.'

Mrs Chandler tensed and her eyes hooded unpleasantly. 'Oh?'

'My name is Sherlock Holmes. I am a private consulting detective.'

Her eyes widened. 'Sherlock Holmes,' she repeated. She had obviously heard of him. Her features darkened. 'What on earth can a private detective want with me?'

'Oh, please, madam, let us not be naïve.'

This remark ruffled her feathers and Mrs Chandler stiffened her back and leaned forward, her eyes fierce and challenging. 'Please state your business, gentlemen. I do not have time for idlers.'

'I am here to trace the mother of one of the babies you... had in your care some eight years ago. A baby you placed with Ronald and Charlotte Temple.'

'Impossible.' The word came sharply like the slamming of a door.

'I want nothing more from you but this information that I am sure you are able to provide. However, if you prevaricate or prove obstructive, I can easily arrange for the full weight of the law to fall upon you and your... your dubious establishment. This is not, I assure you, a veiled threat. It is an open one and easily implemented.'

At this statement, issued by Holmes in a cold measured tone with a definite edge of menace, Mrs Chandler blanched, her hands fluttering over the desk like nervous butterflies.

'I cannot help you,' she said, regaining her composure. 'We do not keep such records. There would be little point. You will appreciate that most women who come to us do not give their real names or other details. They don't wish to be traced.'

'I am sure you will remember this case. The young boy was named William by the Temples. He had a birthmark resembling a pyramid.'

The eyes flickered with recognition, but Mrs Chandler shook her head. 'Eight years is a long time. Many children pass through our hands with all kinds of blemishes and marks on their shoulders, faces, everywhere. When you've been in this business as long as I have they all merge into one – or into none.' She was growing in confidence now and rose from her chair. 'You are, I am afraid, on a wild goose chase, Mr Holmes, and I am unable to accompany you.'

'Unable or unwilling?'

'I must ask you to leave now. I am very busy…'

She moved briskly to the door and opened it. We left without a word.

'She is lying,' said Holmes, once we were outside the building.

'That was my impression.'

'That was my deduction. Note how easily she referred to the possibility of the birthmark being on the boy's shoulder, quickly adding other locations to cover her faux pas. And did you not observe the cabinets further down the hallway?'

'I must confess that I did not.'

'Several wooden cabinets. Filing cabinets, I'll stake my life on it. And what do you find in filing cabinets? Files. Information. Records. No doubt one of those cabinets would offer up the information we require, but I doubt Mrs Chandler would need to refer to it. I am certain it is lodged here.' He tapped the side of his head. 'She clearly remembered the boy, and his birthmark.'

'What now?' I asked as I clambered back inside our waiting cab.

'Back to Baker Street and a short respite from our duties. Tea and a sleep, for we have important work to carry out tonight.'

Seven

Mrs Chandler's visitors had not been out of the building more than five minutes before she was making a telephone call.

'Yes?'

'It's Mrs Chandler.'

'Yes.'

'There's trouble.'

'Go on.'

'I've had a visit from Sherlock Holmes.'

'Have you now.'

'He was asking about the boy. He must be on the case.'

'That is unfortunate. What did you tell him?'

'Nothing. What do you take me for? But he won't be satisfied with my claims of ignorance. I could see that he didn't believe me.'

'Of course not. It is rather unfortunate that he had to get involved. No doubt the Temples have engaged his services to find the child. Oh, well, we will deal with Mr Holmes. Action will have to be taken.'

'Action?'

'He'll have to be disposed of.'

'And as soon as possible, if you want my advice.'

'I think I can live without your advice, Mrs Chandler, but certainly I shall have to act quickly. I am well aware that Mr Holmes is a force to be reckoned with. The sooner he is dealt with the better. Leave the matter with me.'

The line went dead. Mrs Chandler slowly replaced the earpiece. Her bright blue eyes clouded with concern. She hoped that was the last of the matter, but something told her that it was not.

The recipient of Mrs Chandler's telephone call left his desk and moved over to the window. He gazed out onto the murky swell of the Thames, which glinted erratically in the dim sunlight. However, he was not admiring the view; his mind was elsewhere. He was devising a means by which to end Sherlock Holmes's career once and for all.

Eight

Dr Watson's Journal

The activity that Sherlock Holmes had planned for us that evening was a spot of burgling. I believe he had a secret passion for this pursuit. It certainly wasn't the first time he had inveigled me into accompanying him to break into premises late at night. It was as though his so upright and moral soul took delight in this nefarious activity, excusing it on the grounds that it was carried out for just and lawful purposes. He often claimed that had he not chosen to fight on the side of the angels, he would have made a very successful criminal.

'If Mrs Chandler refuses to provide us with the information we require, we must take it for ourselves. We need to gain access to those cabinets,' he assured me as he outlined his plans for that night's activity. He broke off suddenly and looked at me seriously. 'I'm sorry, old fellow, I am afraid I am rather taking your involvement for granted. I assumed that you would want to accompany me tonight. I had no right to do so.' He gave me one of his strange, twisted grins. 'It is not obligatory.'

'You know that I have reservations about such ventures, but nevertheless... I wouldn't miss it for the world.'

'Good man,' he beamed. 'I thought I knew my Watson. So, we leave Baker Street just before midnight. I have all the appropriate tools to ease our entry, but it will be a tricky exercise. There will be infants on the premises and no doubt someone will be about to serve their nocturnal needs. Fortunately, as far as I was able to ascertain from our visit today, the nursing quarters are nowhere near Mrs Chandler's office and the corridor that houses those precious cabinets. We need to locate the papers relating to the year 1887 and then it should not take us long to secure the information that we need.'

I nodded solemnly, but said nothing. Holmes was more sanguine about the success of our mission than I was. He had the remarkable facility of suppressing his imagination on such occasions and focusing solely on the task in view. On the other hand, my mind concocted various obstacles and problems, dramatic scenarios that would hinder or even foil our efforts. These thoughts I kept to myself.

At the appointed hour we left our quarters and walked the length of Baker Street before hailing a cab. We had the driver take us to within half a mile of our destination and then made the rest of the way to the Chandler establishment on foot.

It was a still but cool night, with the pavements damp from an earlier shower. We walked in silence, apart from our footsteps, which rang out in an eerie staccato fashion in the empty streets.

'From our visit this morning I observed that there was a small window at the side of the house that should give us easy access,' said Holmes, his voice now little more than a whisper as we stood in the shadows across the street from the house. The building seemed to be in complete darkness: there was no glimmer of light from any of the windows and it stood like a dark monolith, silhouetted against the midnight sky. Luckily for us the thoroughfare was dimly lighted and there was only the sliver of a crescent moon, which kept disappearing behind a trail of ragged clouds. Stealthily we slipped across the street, and made our way down the side of the building.

'This is it,' Holmes said, pointing to a small casement window, some five feet from the ground. He knelt down and opened a canvas bag containing his burgling tools. He extracted a large chisel. 'I'll see if I can prise it open; smashing the glass would be too noisy.'

I nodded in agreement.

'I think I would gain greater purchase if I were on a level with the window. So if you'll do me the honours, old chap.'

With a grimace, I bent down and Holmes clambered on my back. 'That's it. Excellent,' he said, as he pulled himself up. In my crouched position I heard him working at the window with the chisel. Despite his careful, deliberate actions, the sounds that he made, floating on the still night air, seemed very loud to me.

'It is a recalcitrant devil,' he observed with some frustration.

Holmes is the lightest of individuals and extremely thin; nevertheless, after a few minutes I felt my back giving way under his weight, which seemed to increase with the length of time and the concentrated efforts he was employing to force the window open. I was just about to ask him to give me a rest when he gave a little cry of satisfaction, which was followed by a short crack and then the sound of splintering wood.

'Steady, Watson, just a few more seconds,' he said, as I heard him slide the window up. Greater pressure was placed on my back as he hauled himself up and over the sill. I felt a wonderful release as his weight lifted and I was able to stand erect again. I looked up to see Holmes's face peering back at me through the open window.

'Phase one completed,' he said. 'Pass up the bag and then I'll give you a hand to haul you in.'

Within seconds I was standing at Holmes's side in the darkened house. We waited for some time, straining our ears to catch any sound or movement, but apart from a clock ticking loudly in a nearby room, the rest was silence.

Holmes extracted a dark lantern from his bag and adjusted the beam. 'According to my limited knowledge of the house, the corridor is this way,' he whispered in my ear, pointing to the right. 'Down here, turn right and then left.'

I nodded. I was happy to rely on his judgement. In the dark I had no idea. Slowly, keeping the beam trained on the ground, we moved in the direction Holmes had suggested. As we turned right at the end of the corridor, I recognised a small bust on a plinth from our visit that morning and realised that we were indeed on the right track. So it turned out to be. Within seconds we had turned into the narrow corridor that housed the three large wooden filing cabinets. Holmes crouched by the first, focusing the beam of the lantern on the drawers. 'There is no indication of their contents,' he hissed.

'Are they locked?'

'I shall soon find out.'

He handed me the lantern and tugged at the top drawer. It did not move. Applying the chisel he was able to make short work of breaking it open. He pulled the drawer out and I could see that it was crammed with papers. Holmes snatched up a handful and examined them.

'Any use?' I asked after a few moments.

'These are the kinds of records we need, but they are the wrong year. Too early. Let me try the next cabinet in the hope that they move on chronologically.'

He repeated the process with the second cabinet, snapping the lock with ease. Again he examined a sheaf of papers. 'Ah, this is more like it. 1886. We are close now.' He passed me the lantern and indicated that I hold it close while he riffled through the next section in the cabinet. His fingers now moved more slowly as he withdrew sheet after sheet to examine them. And then he gave a sharp exhalation. 'Here we are, Watson: Temple. Mrs and Mrs. October 1887. Their case notes.' He ripped the sheet from the drawer and secreted it in his overcoat pocket. He turned to me and grinned. As he did so, a loud explosion and a flash of light emanated from the far end of the corridor. Something whizzed past my face and experience told me that it was a bullet.

The next few moments are still confused in my mind as I try to delineate all that happened with such speed and drama. The shock of being shot at almost caused me to drop the lantern, but fortunately I had enough presence of mind to cling on to it. Not only that but I had the sense to turn the beam in the direction from which the shot had been fired. What it illuminated gave my heart a jolt. About twelve feet away was a giant of a man, like some creature from a Grimm's fairy tale. Harshly lit by the lantern's wavering beam, he appeared to be well over six feet tall and built like a buffalo. His face was remarkably round and red and encased by a riot of unruly hair and beard. He could well have just emerged from a prehistoric cave. However, what was perhaps more daunting than his bulk and the ferocious grimace on his frighteningly ugly face was the fact that he held a very large pistol in his hand and it was aimed at me. I cannot claim that my next move was calculated or even considered. It occurred instinctively:

an innate reaction of self-preservation. I took a step forward and flashed the beam of the lantern straight into his face. He squinted and he gave a brief groan of discomfort as, blinded by the light, his shot went wide.

With a roar, he advanced on us. Holmes went forward to meet him with such speed that the ogre had no time to aim the pistol before my friend plunged the chisel deep into his breast. He uttered an inhuman, almost bovine bellow, a strange mixture of surprise and fury. While he was distracted by the pain and shock of his wound, Holmes was able to grab the gun from his hand before retreating. The chisel remained stuck in the man's chest, a dark stain spreading around it. With another roar, he wrenched the chisel from its resting place and flung it to the ground. He then began to lumber towards us.

'Run,' Holmes cried, as he fired off a warning shot. I needed no further bidding and I hared down the hallway with Holmes close at my heels. By now there were voices raised elsewhere in the house. As we reached the window by which we had gained access, there were shadowy figures appearing from all directions, some carrying oil lamps, bobbing amber spots of light in the gloom. More shots were fired. As I clambered over the window ledge, I saw our giant assailant grab hold of Holmes, haul him off the ground and begin to shake him as though he were a rag doll. Then there was another shot and the creature cried out in pain once more and instantly released his grip on my friend. Both men crumpled to the floor, but Holmes was quickly on his feet again and followed me out of the window. We landed in an ungainly fashion on the ground below.

Someone in the darkness cried out, 'Stop, you devils!' and two further shots were fired. Once out of the building, we ran as fast as we could into the maze of streets. We kept going for about ten minutes until, completely out of breath, I begged Holmes that we stop for a while.

We both stood panting in the doorway of a tobacconist's shop. I thought Holmes sounded particularly wheezy until I realised he was laughing in that strange, almost silent fashion of his.

'We shifted from melodrama to farce, eh, Watson? All we needed was Messrs Gilbert and Sullivan to set tonight's adventure to music and we would have a fine comic opera.'

'We nearly got killed,' I replied, sternly, failing to see the humorous aspect of the situation.

'Such circumstances always add a little extra spice to an investigation. It was obvious that we were expected. Mrs Chandler, or more likely her master, never intended for us to leave those premises alive. Hence the presence of the Neanderthal nightwatchman armed with a pistol. Not the usual sort of guardian in a nursery. And you saw those others coming to his aid. The place was full of armed men, waiting for us.'

'He was a frightful creature. He looked like something out of a circus sideshow. Is he dead?'

'I fear so. When he grabbed me, there was only one way I was going to escape and that was to shoot him. If I had not pulled the trigger when I did, he would no doubt have broken my neck.' He paused for a moment, features taking on a more sombre expression. 'Ah, Watson, this kidnapping case is taking on a very dark hue and I suspect it will grow a great deal darker before we get to the bottom of it.'

Nine

The grey light of dawn was struggling to make its presence felt in the dingy attic room. Everything seemed to be washed in a stale muddy monochrome; even the boy curled up on the makeshift bed blended into the grey sacking that half-covered his body. His eyes were closed and his small frame rose and fell gently as he slept.

'Has he been drugged?' These were the first words the dark gentleman uttered as he entered the room. He saw no necessity for the nicety of a greeting. These were hired hands who, under other circumstances, would not be allowed within ten feet of him. They were paid for their services. That was all the recognition they needed.

Annie Grimes rose awkwardly to her feet. 'He has, sir, but it weren't an easy task. He's not been taking his food. Got a good spirit has the lad. We had to force the potion down him. It was in a pot of hot milk, but he tried hard to spit it out. Still...' She paused for a conspiratorial smile before continuing. 'Still, we persevered.'

She nodded towards the child. 'He's dead to the world, now. Ain't he, Percy?'

Percy, who had been hovering in the shadows, stepped forward at the mention of his name. 'Dead to the world he is, right enough, sir. Ready for the journey.'

The dark gentleman gave a brief nod. 'I have the carriage waiting outside. Bring the boy down.'

Some moments later Percy Grimes carried the drugged youth, wrapped in a rough woollen blanket, out to the waiting carriage.

'Lay him on the seat inside. I'll watch over him during the journey,' said the dark gentleman as he opened the carriage door.

'Right you are.' Grimes did as he was bidden. The boy stirred fitfully and his eyelids flickered momentarily, but once his head was resting on the carriage seat he slipped back into deep slumber.

'That will be all for now,' said the dark gentleman, flipping a sovereign in the direction of Grimes, who caught it with practised ease. 'I will be in touch when I require your services again.'

'Much obliged, sir,' replied Grimes, touching his forelock. Such an action was against the grain, but he knew that playing the part of a humble and obedient servant might very well gain him further employment and as he had observed to Annie, 'The dark gentleman pays a good whack.'

With a cry of 'drive on', the carriage door slammed shut and the vehicle lurched forward, quickly gaining speed.

For some moments Grimes stared after the departing carriage and then he spat in the gutter.

Ten

Dr Watson's Journal

The next day I rose somewhat later than is my usual custom. I was more than a little fatigued by the events of the previous night. I kept forgetting that I was no longer the lithe young man who had travelled to Afghanistan with the 5th Northumberland Fusiliers. I prided myself that I kept reasonably fit, but however hard one tries, one cannot hold back middle age.

On entering our sitting room, I discovered Holmes at the table, his old clay pipe clamped in his mouth and his brow furrowed as he studied some sheets of paper. It was clear from the debris on the table that he had breakfasted some time ago.

He glanced up at my approach. 'Ah, my dear fellow, how are you this morning?'

'A little stiff and tired.'

'Hot coffee and some of Mrs Hudson's bacon and scrambled eggs should soon help revive you and put that old spring back in your step.' He favoured me with a brief smile before returning to his perusal of the papers before him.

I took up his suggestion and some fifteen minutes later I was tucking into our landlady's delightful comestibles. I had not realised how hungry I was. When I pushed away the empty plate and drained my coffee cup, I felt a hundred per cent better than I had done when I'd dragged myself out of bed.

I turned to my friend, who had been smoking quietly with his eyes staring dreamily at the ceiling. I knew this mood. He was deep in thought, weighing facts against possibilities, comparing the evidence we possessed with various theories.

'What have you learned from those documents we obtained last night?' I asked, and I could not resist adding, 'The ones that nearly cost us our lives.'

Holmes lifted three sheets of paper from the table and let them fall from his grasp. 'They tell us little but provide one vital piece of information: the name of the woman who brought the baby, the little boy with the triangular birthmark, to Mrs Chandler: Alice Sunderland.'

'Is there an address?'

'There is a street. Bat Street. No number.'

'Bat Street?'

'Whitechapel.'

'Not a very salubrious area.'

'Indeed. But considering the circumstances concerning the child, I hardly expected anything else. It could, I suppose, have been the child of a servant who needed to get rid of it in order to retain her position in a respectable household, but the Whitechapel address implies it is more likely that the boy is the offspring of a street woman.'

'They have notoriously brief lives,' I observed. 'Few live to be more than forty years of age, riddled with disease of all humours. It is a wretched existence.'

Holmes nodded. 'I well remember the poor women we encountered during the time of the Ripper murders.'

I saw the sadness in his eyes as he thought back to those sad, grotesquely painted, essentially fragile creatures who haunted the streets of Whitechapel. They were the prey of the drunkard's blow, the pimp's ill-treatment, disease, hunger and at that time, the Ripper's blade also.

'And this woman, this Alice Sunderland, if she is one of those unfortunates, it is unlikely that she will still be living in Bat Street after all this time.'

'Indeed. Our lead is fragile in the extreme. She could be dead or have moved on. We shall just have to test the waters.'

'When do you intend to visit Whitechapel?'

'The place comes alive – if that is the phrase I want – at night. I suggest an early evening saunter along those benighted streets.'

I had intended to have a light lunch and take an afternoon nap before our evening excursion in an effort to fully recover from our adventures of the previous night. However my plans were disturbed by the arrival of a visitor. Mrs Hudson bore up his card on a tray, and Holmes glanced at it and handed it to me with a sardonic chuckle.

The card read: 'Inspector Dominic Gaunt, Metropolitan Police, Scotland Yard, London'.

'Since when have the police been issued with visiting cards?' I asked.

'I think this is a personal affectation. Inspector Gaunt appears to be one of the newer breed of inspectors that our old friend

Lestrade has told us about: a little too pompous and arrogant for their own good. At least that's Lestrade's view. Now we can judge for ourselves.'

Our visitor entered our sitting room a few moments later. He was a tall, impressive figure, athletic in build with square handsome features and a thick mane of black hair. He was impeccably dressed and had keen, intelligent eyes. This policeman was certainly a contrast to the rather shabby, shambling figure of our rat-faced friend Giles Lestrade.

'Mr Holmes, it is a great pleasure and honour to meet you,' he said, his voice rich and deep with a slight hint of an Irish accent. He grasped my friend's hand and shook it warmly.

Holmes smiled and nodded his head. 'It is always a pleasure to meet a member of Her Majesty's police force. You will know that this is my friend and colleague, Dr Watson.'

'Sir,' he said, turning to me in acknowledgement, but I was denied the privilege of a handshake.

'Pray take a seat and tell us what brings you to our door, Inspector,' said Holmes, indicating a chair. Inspector Gaunt did as he was asked.

'I come to you concerning a rather delicate manner, Mr Holmes. I am currently in charge of the Temple kidnapping investigation.' He paused and cast a searching glance at my friend, whose face remained a neutral mask. 'It has come to my attention,' continued Gaunt with a certain amount of awkwardness, 'that you are also carrying out your own enquiries concerning this case.'

'Oh,' said Holmes, casually, 'and how have you come into possession of such information?'

Gaunt hesitated. It seemed as though he was trying to decide how to respond to Holmes's question. However, my friend did it for him.

'No need to prevaricate, Inspector. You no doubt were told by your surveillance officer, who is positioned not far from the Temple residence's entrance gate. I observed him yesterday when we paid a visit there. If my memory serves me right – and it usually does – he was dressed as some kind of artisan with a bag of tools.'

At first Gaunt seemed surprised at this revelation and then his face softened into a smile. 'You are quite right, sir,' he said. 'The fellow you refer to is one of my men.'

'Mr Temple has no doubt expressed his dismay at the police's progress in this investigation and when your keen-eyed spy saw us arriving at the house, it would be easy to surmise that we had been engaged to supplement the official enquiry.'

'Indeed. And as you intimate we have made scant progress in this affair. Both the boy and his abductors seem to have vanished off the face of the earth.' Gaunt ran his fingers thorough his luxuriant hair. 'That's why I am here to enquire if you have made any headway with the matter. We should work together rather than separately…'

Holmes held up his hand to silence the policeman. 'I am afraid, Inspector, it is a cast-iron rule of mine that I work alone in the interest of my client. It is only at the moment of climax that I am prepared to call in Scotland Yard.'

'But surely our combined efforts…'

Holmes shook his head. 'If I had wanted to be part of the Metropolitan machine I should have enlisted in the force.'

'But if you have any pertinent information, surely you would be prepared to share it?'

'Possibly. But at present I have gleaned nothing that could be of any use to you. It seems that we are both staring into the darkness hoping to catch a gleam of light. I am afraid that I cannot help you.'

Gaunt's features darkened and his eyes blazed with suppressed anger. 'Cannot or will not?' he snapped.

Holmes made a dismissive gesture with his hand, prompting our visitor to rise abruptly from the chair. 'I had expected more of you, Mr Holmes,' he said with some heat. 'There is a little boy's life at stake. I would have thought that issue was paramount...'

'Indeed it is. And I can assure you that all my endeavours are focussed on that problem.'

'But you are not prepared to share your findings.'

'My findings, such as they are, are currently of no use to Scotland Yard. When the path becomes clearer and a solution is in sight, that is the time I will turn to the official police force.'

'Then, I shall take up no more of your valuable time.' This statement was issued through gritted teeth. Gaunt strode to the door and flung it open before turning to face us once more.

'Good day, gentlemen,' he rasped before slamming the door shut.

Holmes gave one of his dry chuckles. 'The arrogance of the man, coming here expecting me to do his work for him.'

'You were a little churlish,' I said.

'Yes, I was, wasn't I? There was something about Inspector Gaunt that I did not take kindly to.'

'Nevertheless we are working for the same goal and you were not truthful with him. We have gleaned some evidence that may be of use to his investigation.'

'And in the hands of the dunderheads at Scotland Yard could lead to catastrophe. The situation is extremely delicate. As Gaunt observed, a young boy's life is in the balance. One careless move could lead to disaster. This matter needs treating with the utmost care and subtlety – qualities that are not prevalent within the confines of Scotland Yard.'

'He seemed such an able fellow.'

'Don't be fooled by a smart suit and a confident manner, Watson. Gaunt did not come here to join forces with us in trying to solve this crime.'

'What for then?'

'To pick my brains. To learn what I knew.'

That evening we set off for Whitechapel. As dusk took hold of this grimy benighted area of London, Holmes and I turned into Bat Street. It was a wider thoroughfare than I had imagined. I had expected it to be a narrow alley of terrace houses, each as anonymous and shabby as the next, with blank grimy windows. I was wrong. It was a broad street with a small butcher's shop, a pawnbroker's and a public house, The Saracen's Head, with a vivid sign advertising its presence. It was lively with pedestrians: there was a blind beggar soliciting alms and a singer grating his way through some unmemorable folk song along with a trio of street girls hanging around under a gas light, more in casual conversation than seeking trade. Holmes approached them and immediately they sensed a possible customer and broke away from the group, each striking what no doubt they considered was a provocative pose. They grinned and preened, waiting, it would seem, for Holmes to make his choice. Each woman was heavily made up so that their faces resembled a child's garish shiny-faced doll. I could not say how old any of them were with accuracy. Certainly they were not in the flush of youth, but their mummified faces hid their true ages.

Holmes touched his hat in greeting. 'I am anxious to discover the whereabouts of Alice Sunderland. I wonder if you ladies are able to help me.'

They giggled at the reference to the term 'ladies' and exchanged dark glances. Holmes held up a shiny coin. 'I am prepared to pay for your trouble.' Six avaricious eyes focussed on the coin.

'What was the name again, duckie?' said the tallest of the group.

'Alice Sunderland.'

The three women exchanged glances again, nudged each other suggestively and laughed. 'I think we could help you, but you see there are three of us. You get my meaning?'

Holmes nodded and withdrew a further two coins.

'That's right handsome of you, sir,' said another, before stifling a giggle.

'I'll take those,' said the tall one, holding out her hand.

'The information first,' said Holmes.

The woman leaned close to him and whispered something in his ear. Holmes's face darkened; his whole expression was one of displeasure. With some reluctance he handed over the coins. The woman curtsied and burst into a fit of laughter and then passed a coin each to her companions, who seemed equally amused.

'Come, Watson,' said Holmes brusquely.

'What on earth was that all about?'

Holmes flashed me a sardonic grin. 'That was all about three street women getting the better of Sherlock Holmes.'

'Do you mean they didn't tell you where Alice Sunderland is?'

'Oh, yes, they told me all right.'

'Well, where is she?'

'Under our very noses,' he replied sourly.

By now we had reached the entrance of The Saracen's Head. Holmes raised his cane and pointed to the small sign above the door that gave details of the proprietor who was licensed to sell beer, spirits and other intoxicating beverages. The name given was Alice Sunderland.

'We had been thinking that Alice Sunderland was a prostitute, when it appears that she is the licensee of a thriving business.' Holmes smiled and gave a dark chuckle. 'If I had been a little more observant, I could have saved myself three sovereigns. Still, it proved a valuable lesson. One that I should have learned years ago: never make assumptions that blind you to other possibilities. Well, old boy, as my purse is somewhat depleted at the moment, the drinks are on you.'

The Saracen's Head was full to bursting with customers. There seemed to be the whole array of London society in the place: a bunch of costermongers; numerous nefarious-looking fellows; a few soldiers; and several small West End types slumming it, using the East End as one of their cabaret stops. And of course there were prostitutes patrolling the clientele, seeking custom or a free drink.

With some effort we made our way to the bar. I ordered two pints of porter from the burly barman. As I paid, Holmes leaned forward and addressed the man. 'Is Alice around?' he asked, his voice coarser than normal. The barman raised a quizzical eyebrow as though he had not heard properly or understood the question.

'Alice Sunderland,' said Holmes.

The barman flipped out a watch from his waistcoat and studied it. 'She'll be on in a few minutes,' he said, before moving down the counter to the next customer.

A small table in the corner had suddenly become vacant and with great alacrity, Holmes and I took possession of it.

'What did he mean?' I asked above the raucous babble that filled the room, as I sat down on a small stool.

'I think we are about to be entertained,' my friend replied, nodding towards the far end of the bar.

It was here the crowd was moving backwards to reveal a small makeshift stage and a battered upright piano, at which sat a large Negro wearing an amorphous white shirt and a bowler hat. He hammered out a set of raucous rallying chords while announcing in a loud, rich voice: 'Pray silence, you lugs, for our own Ally Sunderland.'

A portly woman wearing what looked suspiciously like a ginger wig clambered up onto the stage. She was dressed in a large glittery gown that was obviously too small for her and as a result strained at every curve and crevice.

'Hello, cheeky boys and girls,' she cried.

The audience roared their approval and the piano struck up with the popular song, 'The "Ticket-of-Leave" Man'. After the first verse most of the customers were joining in. I glanced over at Holmes, who maintained a tight amused grin.

Two more rousing songs followed and the crowd were now fully entranced by the performance. Then 'Our Ally' gave the touching ballad, 'Alice, Where Art Thou?' which brought a respectful hush from the throng. Her act concluded with an energetic rendition of 'The Underground Railway'. As she finished, the whole audience roared their approval.

'Is this the Alice Sunderland we are seeking, Holmes?' I asked.

'I see no reason why it should not be. It is time for us to find out.' Without another word he was out of his seat and pushing his way through the crowd of admirers that clustered around Alice Sunderland. She seemed both delighted and amused by their open admiration. With great guile, Holmes managed to sidle right up to her and whisper in her ear. At once the broad smile that had adorned her plump features disappeared. Her eyes widened in shock and for a moment she stared at my friend without saying a word. He spoke to her again and at length she responded, shaking her head in denial, all the while her eyes darting around the room. Holmes had further words in her ear, to which, with some reluctance, she responded. Holmes nodded and moved away as surreptitiously as he had arrived. Within seconds, Alice Sunderland was beaming again and chatting with her admirers, but this time her jollity did not reach her eyes, which now registered fear and worry.

'I think I have disturbed the lady, Watson, which shows that we are on the right track,' my friend informed me on reaching my side.

'What did she say?'

'Not much, but she looked suitably distressed when I told her I wanted to talk to her about the child she sent to the baby farm eight years ago. She tried to deny it but I told her that I had proof from Mrs Chandler herself. That convinced our "Ally". She said she couldn't talk now, but invited me back when the pub closes around midnight.' My friend rubbed his hands. 'That should be a very interesting and enlightening interview.'

Eleven

❧

Dr Watson's Journal

We could hear Big Ben chiming midnight as we approached The Saracen's Head once more, later that night. The streets were much quieter now, but there was still a number of folk about: drunks, prostitutes and potential clients along with knots of late-night revellers and in the occasional doorway some poor homeless wretch curled up for the night. One got the impression that in this part of London it never grew quiet: there was always some activity.

'Our hostess said that she would leave the door of the saloon bar on the latch so that we could enter without knocking,' said Holmes. Through the frosted glass at the windows, we could see the dim illumination within as though one or two lights were still burning.

On entering the building, the smell of stale tobacco, sweat and sour ale assailed the nostrils. A thin curtain of smoke still hung in the air so that it was like viewing the place through a fine gauze veil. There was a shadow moving over by the bar and as we progressed further into the room we saw that it was an old man with stooped shoulders who was wiping down the counter. He glanced up briefly at our approach.

'We have come to see Alice Sunderland,' said Holmes.

'Her ladyship's up them stairs,' the fellow replied gruffly, returning to his cleaning duties.

We passed through a door marked 'Private' at the far end of the bar and ascended a narrow staircase and on to a dimly lighted landing along which was a door partly ajar. A strange shimmering light emanated from the chamber beyond. As Holmes laid his finger on the door, I sensed his body stiffen. 'There is something wrong,' he whispered to me, as he pushed the door open.

There *was* something wrong: lying back on a chaise longue illuminated by flickering candlelight was the body of Alice Sunderland, her head lolling backwards. The hilt of a dagger rose from her chest, surrounded by a small patch of coagulated blood. Holmes sprang forward, felt her pulse and then turned to me sharply. 'See to her, Watson. All is not lost.' With these words he dashed from the room and I heard him race down the stairs.

I turned my attention to the lady. I too felt her pulse. It was very weak and irregular but still in evidence. As gently as I could I raised her into a sitting position and then bathed her brow with a damp flannel I secured from a wash basin in the corner of the room. Her eyelids fluttered and gradually opened. Even then I knew this was a temporary state of affairs – a last rallying call. It was clear to me that her attacker had been successful in bringing this lady's life to a close. She gazed at me uncomprehendingly and tried to speak, but the words would not come.

'I'll get you some water,' I said and she nodded her head imperceptibly.

'Gin, if you please,' she muttered, the words emanating in a harsh whisper. 'Give me gin.'

I was certainly not going to deny a dying woman her last request so I looked around the room for a bottle of gin. I spied one on a small table by the door. Moments later I was administering the drink to her. She sipped gently, a slight smile touching her lips. 'Lovely,' she said.

Some moments later Holmes returned to my side. 'The devil got away,' he cried, his whole body heaving with the exertions of the chase. 'How is she?'

I shook my head. Holmes emitted a groan and knelt down by Alice Sunderland.

'It is Sherlock Holmes,' he said, his voice kind, but I who knew him well could detect that steely note of urgency there also. 'What can you tell me about the Temple child? He has been taken. We need to save his life.'

For a moment the dying woman closed her eyes and when she opened them they were filled with tears. 'He is a precious child. Royal.'

'Royal,' I cried.

'Yes. He is the child of Mary Kelly and Eddy.'

Holmes cast me a swift glance. 'Eddy, the late Duke of Clarence, son of the Prince of Wales.'

'Yes,' she affirmed, her voice growing fainter until it was a mere whisper. 'They were married and had a child. A little boy. A prince.'

'Mary Kelly... she was one of the Ripper's victims...' I murmured as the seriousness of the situation slowly began to unfold in my mind.

Alice Sunderland nodded her head wearily. 'The Ripper was

their weapon to get to Mary and then to the boy. They wanted him dead.'

'Who are they?'

The dying woman gave a gurgling laugh. 'Who do you think? Mary came to me and begged me to take the child, to get him to safety. She knew her days were numbered. How could I refuse?' The tears rolled freely down her ashen face. 'I couldn't keep the boy here. Not in the heart of Whitechapel. They'd soon get wind of him here.'

'So you took him to Mrs Chandler's baby farm and put him up for adoption.'

Alice nodded. 'All I cared about – all Mary cared about – was that the boy would live. She didn't care about his royal heritage. That counted for nothing. I thought he was safe... but they've caught up with him at last.'

'Who are they?' Holmes repeated gently.

The woman's eyes flickered and closed momentarily before opening again. They were now less bright, less focused. The light of life was fading in them.

'I reckon you know as well as I do, Mr Sherlock Holmes.' She smiled and then her head lolled to one side, her eyes closing for the last time.

'My God, Holmes,' I said at length, 'what does it all mean?'

'That is something I intend to find out, my friend. The tentacles of this dark and dangerous business are spread far and wide. One thing is clear: we are dealing with a sinister and treacherous organisation and they know we are on their trail. It did not take them long to silence this poor creature. They knew she held information that was vital to us.'

I glanced down at the bloody corpse of Alice Sunderland, saw the gruesome handiwork of our enemies, and shuddered. 'What are we to do about her?' I asked, covering the woman's face up with a cloth.

'We'll find a bobby on the beat and tell him the basic facts and leave it in his hands to see to the rest.'

An hour later we were back in Baker Street sitting either side of the glowing embers of our fire, each with a glass of brandy in our hands.

'Who killed Alice Sunderland?' I asked.

'Well, it was the fellow who appeared to be cleaning up in the bar when we arrived.'

'He was an old chap.'

'So he seemed. As a practitioner of disguise myself, I should have been more wary. When we went upstairs, he was off like the wind. He had to have had a great head start for me to fail to catch up with him, but I can assure you that he was no old man.'

'And you have no idea who the fellow was.'

'Specifically, no. But he is obviously one of the minions who are part of the organising force behind this whole affair. A fine set of fellows all: we have the kidnappers, the brute who attacked us and would have killed us at the Chandler establishment, and the murderer of Alice Sunderland.'

'And what is the motive? What is their goal?'

'Of that I am not absolutely sure, although I have my theories.'

'And what is all this about Eddy, the late Duke of Clarence?'

'There lies the nub of the matter.' Holmes rolled his brandy glass between his hands. 'There was an idea, a theory that was circulating in the higher echelons of Scotland Yard at the time of Jack the Ripper, that the Queen's grandson, the Prince of Wales's son, Prince Albert Victor Christian Edward, the Duke of Clarence and Avondale, known as "Eddy" to his familiars, was in some way connected with the murders.'

'What! How preposterous.'

Holmes smiled. 'Ah, you old royalist. When will you learn that he who wears the crown does not necessarily have a noble heart?'

'I cannot believe...'

'Maybe not. And it was clear that Eddy could not have been the Ripper. He was away from London on at least one occasion when the killer struck.'

'Well then...'

'But,' Holmes raised his index finger in an admonishing gesture, 'that does not mean he was not in some way connected with those terrible crimes.'

'In some way...? What on earth do you mean?'

Holmes stroked his chin thoughtfully. 'There was a conspiracy of silence at Scotland Yard during that very dark period. As you will remember I was only involved at the periphery of the investigation. Sir Charles Warren made sure I was kept at arm's length. He wanted to make sure that I was denied access to a great deal of the evidence that Inspector Abberline and his men had collected.'

'I remember. You were frustrated that you had been sidelined.'

'Indeed. But it wasn't arrogance or jealousy on their part as it had been in some instances in the past. It was because they knew that if I had been given all the facts, I could have solved the case and unmasked the identity of Jack the Ripper.'

Holmes had never discussed the case with me so frankly. I remembered how brooding and sullen he had been at the time, but he had never confided in me. I could see now from his strained, gaunt features that the memory of his treatment still caused him anger and distress.

'With what fragments of information I managed to glean, I constructed several theories. The key to the murders was the uncovering of the motive. Were we really dealing with a clever madman who, in the popular parlance of the time, "had a grudge against whores", or was there a more sinister and subtle purpose behind the crimes? The fact that the name of a member of the royal family was even breathed, whispered in connection with the Ripper killings, was remarkable and this intrigued me. I asked myself, why? Although the man himself, Eddy, could not have actually committed the crimes because he had royal engagements on at least two of the nights when the murders took place, it seemed to me that there could be some kind of link between him and the deaths of these unfortunate women.'

'You never breathed a word to me about this.'

'There was no point until I had proof. But all my enquiries were met with silence. Well, more than silence. I was warned off by no less a figure than Sir Charles Warren himself. He informed me that if I persisted in that particular line of enquiry, I would be arrested on some trumped-up charge and incarcerated. There was no subtlety or sophistry in this warning. It was an open, clear threat.'

At this statement, I felt my blood run cold. That such a high ranking public figure as Sir Charles Warren could act in such a way was shocking in the extreme. 'That is outrageous!' I cried.

'Outrageous, but informative.'

'Informative?'

'Does not his putting a stop to my investigation into the royal connection suggest that there was one? Otherwise, why curtail my activities? He was frightened that I would find out the truth.'

'And what is the truth?'

'I didn't know then, but now recent events have helped to

raise one of the veils obscuring the matter. Consider what Alice Sunderland told us. Mary Kelly, the last Ripper victim, entered into some form of marriage with Eddy and bore him a male child. That placed her in a vulnerable position for the baby was heir to the throne of Great Britain, after the Prince of Wales.'

'My God! A harlot's child.'

'It stands to reason that some members of the establishment were charged to get rid of both mother and child. Wipe them from the face of the earth and all those who knew of their secret in order to protect the crown.'

'It is fantastic. So you think these street women, the victims of the Ripper, were slaughtered because of what they knew?'

Holmes nodded. 'The knowledge of the marriage and the existence of the boy child. It seems clear that they were using the women to search for Mary Kelly. You may remember that her death, the final killing, was the most vicious and obscene of them all.'

'Indeed,' I said. Even as a medical man who had seen the horrors of war and treated the most terrible wounds out in Afghanistan, my stomach had turned when I read the dreadful details of Mary Kelly's death. Her body had been eviscerated, her face hacked away, and her heart had been ripped from her body and taken away by the killer. Even now as I write about it, my gorge rises at the thought of such a foul deed.

'Fortunately for the boy, they never made the link between Mary and Alice Sunderland, who had the great presence of mind to get the child away from Whitechapel as soon as possible.'

'She took him to Chandler's baby farm where he became just another anonymous unwanted baby.'

Holmes took a large sip of brandy, rolling the liquid around his mouth, before responding. 'Yes. The mother died, but the baby survived. Somehow, someone has discovered the identity and the whereabouts of the child...'

'The boy adopted as William Temple.'

'And so, like the behemoth, the threat to the monarchy has reared its head from the murky waters once more.'

I shook my head sadly. 'And now they have got him, they will surely have killed him.'

Holmes gazed into the fading embers of our fire with a faraway look in his eyes. 'It may not be as simple as that, Watson. It all depends on who "they" are and what their motive is. One thing is certain, however: this time I will follow this investigation to the end and nothing – or no one – will stop me.'

Twelve

When William woke up he found he was in a proper bed. His head lay on a soft pillow and cool cotton sheets pressed gently down on him. For one wonderful moment he thought that he was back in his own bed at home. He sat up in some excitement with a grin, but it faded quickly, for as he gazed around him expecting familiar surroundings, he realised that he was in a chamber that he had never seen before. It was well appointed with rich furnishings and a fire burned brightly in the grate. The lights were low and the flames sent sinister shadows dancing across the ornate ceiling. Seated in a chair near his bed was an elderly lady who, until his sudden movement disturbed her, had been knitting quietly. Now she sat forward and turned her attention to him.

'Master William,' she said gently. 'You are awake.'

'Where am I? I want to go home.'

The lady smiled as she rose and moved to the wall by the bed and tugged at the bell rope. 'You *are* home, young sir. Home where you belong,' she said.

'This is not my home,' the boy cried defiantly, throwing back the bedclothes.

'Now, don't be troublesome. We don't want to have to put you to sleep again. Be a good boy and all will be well.'

William's eyes darted around the room. The door seemed to shimmer and shift in the shadowy firelight like a tempting mirage. To get to it, he would have to pass the old woman. She noticed his frantic darting glances and guessed his intentions. Her body stiffened and her features darkened. Gone was the benign smile and placid demeanour to be replaced by the harsh blinking ferocity of a hawk.

'Get back into bed, Master William.' The words emerged in a fierce staccato rhythm.

The boy had no intention of obeying her. However, just as he was about to make a break for freedom, the door of the room opened and a tall man appeared. With swift strides he made his way towards the boy.

'What's this?' the dark man said, not unkindly. 'Out of bed?'

'I want to go home,' cried the boy, his voice cracking and tears starting to trickle down his face. The dark man leaned forward and put his arm around the boy's shoulder.

'There,' he said softly. 'You cry if you want to. You have had a difficult time. But you are safe now and will be cared for. There is no need to fret. You are in no danger.'

'I want my mother.'

The man shook his head. 'That is not possible, William. You are going to have to be strong. I am afraid I have to tell you that you will never see your mother and father again. You know, of course, they were not your real mother and father. They were only looking after you for a time. In preparation for your destiny.'

The boy continued to sob until he slumped to the floor, his emotions having exhausted him.

'It is my duty to look after you now. You are a very special boy, William. Did you know that?'

He lifted the crying child and laid him on the bed. 'Sleep now. All will seem so much better in the morning. With some warm food inside you, the world will seem a kinder place.'

'I want my mother,' moaned the boy.

The man threw the bedclothes over the child. 'Call Smithers if there is any trouble,' he said to the woman. 'I must get back to London. I have work to do.'

Thirteen

Dr Watson's Journal

Despite being completely fatigued, I slept badly that night. My mind was crammed with a variety of disparate thoughts about the dangerous affair we were investigating. Memories of the Ripper killings, mingled with images from our previous evening's adventures, which in turn were mixed up with the contemplations concerning the Duke of Clarence and the kidnapped boy. Dawn was already making its presence felt before I was able to slip into a reasonably untroubled sleep.

As a result of my fitful slumber, I rose late. As I attended to my toilet, I wondered what course of action Holmes intended to take next. He had not mentioned his future plans to me as we sat before the dying fire, drinking brandy and discussing the case. On reaching our sitting room I found him at the breakfast table studying a sheet of note paper. He gave me a nod of greeting and passed the sheet to me.

'This arrived this morning. It was posted through our letter box.'

I KNOW WHERE THE BOY IS. I CAN HELP YOU.
MEET ME AT THE LORD NELSON, CHRISTOPHER
DOCKS AT TEN THIS EVENING. COME ALONE.

A FRIEND

I gazed at the paper for some moments. 'Can this be genuine?'
I asked at length.

Holmes chuckled. 'Genuine bait, I suspect. The spiders are
trying to lure the fly.'

'You will not go.'

'I must. How can I not?'

'But you have acknowledged that this is a trap.'

'A potential trap – if I am foolish enough to fall into it. In many
ways this message is encouraging.'

'In what way?' I said with surprise.

'They are worried about my intervention. I pose a threat to
them and so they wish to eliminate me.'

'And that is encouraging?'

'It means I am getting too close for their comfort. They are
worried I will scupper their plans.'

'But you won't go tonight.'

'Oh, yes, I shall. But not without precautions.'

'What precautions?'

'I will let you know later. Suffice it to say, if you are willing, you
will be part of my arrangements.'

'I am always willing to help, you know that. But I would advise
you not to be reckless enough to respond to this summons. They
are obviously cunning creatures.'

'And so am I. I can count on you then?'

'Of course.'

Holmes gave me a broad smile and touched my shoulder. 'In all my investigations, you are the one fixed point, Watson, and for that I am very grateful.' So saying he rose quickly and without another word disappeared into his bedroom.

He did not emerge for about half an hour. When the door eventually opened, it was no longer my friend Sherlock Holmes who stood on the threshold, but rather an aged, round-shouldered, rough-looking cove in a shabby pea jacket and a peaked sailor's cap pulled down in a jaunty fashion across his brow. The face was adorned with an explosion of white whiskers and a thin black pipe hung from his mouth. I had ceased being surprised by the way Holmes was able to adopt a disguise, for I had seen him do it many times in the course of our detective work together, but I never lost that sense of wonder at the way he was able to transform himself with such skill and authenticity into a range of characters whose form and persona were so different to his own. Here before me was an aged salt with a slightly bowlegged gait and ruddy complexion bearing no similarity to the lean, ascetic detective whom I had observed not thirty minutes before.

The figure touched his cap in greeting. 'Able Seaman Bird at your service, sir. Just finished a stretch on the *Alexandria*: long trip from the Azores. I'm just goin' to have a shamble around the Christopher Docks to see if there are any bunks agoin' for my next jaunt.'

I burst out laughing at this stellar performance. 'You want to be careful, or you may find yourself press-ganged aboard some vessel,' I grinned.

'I am always careful,' said Holmes with some solemnity. 'Hold yourself in readiness for tonight. I shall return in due course.'

Fourteen

&

L ater that afternoon in an anonymous office in one of the
government buildings in Whitehall, Mycroft Holmes, the
detective's brother and lynchpin of the British government,
received a very distinguished visitor.

'You are no doubt aware of the reason for my visit,' said the
Prime Minister, seating himself in the comfortable armchair
opposite Mycroft's desk.

'I expected you earlier, sir, or at least to be summoned to your
presence,' said the large man, wafting grains of snuff from the
folds of his waistcoat. 'I knew it was a case of Mohammed and the
mountain. I was unsure who would visit whom.'

The Prime Minister gave a weary half-smile. 'Let us dispense
with whimsical semantics, Mycroft. This matter is too serious for
such niceties.'

Mycroft gave a nod.

'You know, of course, that your brother Sherlock is now
involved in the matter.'

Mycroft sighed. 'Trust Sherlock to enmesh himself in something like this. He has a talent for it.'

'There is no doubt that he is a brilliant man and seeing that now our enemies are on his track, it would be politic and beneficial to involve him formally. Of course this will mean he will have to be informed of all the facts at our disposal. It is not an ideal situation, but we cannot expect the man to function effectively if he is ignorant of the relevant details, no matter how sensitive they are. He must be told. That is your task. It is possible that he may be able to shine a light on our difficulties.'

'I agree up to a point. You will be well aware that my brother does not take kindly to instruction. It is essential to him that he retains his independence at all times.'

'We can allow him a little rope, but this matter is so delicate that it may well be disastrous to allow him a completely unfettered rein.'

Mycroft rubbed his chin and sighed. 'Easier to say than to bring into practice.'

'That is your responsibility, Mycroft. Everything in our power must be done to erase this terrible threat. The monarchy and the government of Great Britain are at risk while this shadow looms over us.'

Mycroft was tempted to chide the Prime Minister for indulging in melodrama, but good sense and discretion prevailed and he said nothing and just delivered the sternest of nods.

'For the moment, the villains of the piece hold the upper hand, a hand with a royal flush in it, so to speak. I, along with Her Majesty's Government and indeed Her Majesty herself, are relying on you. Is that understood?'

'Indeed.'

'Very well. Keep me informed at all times.' The Prime Minister rose regally from the chair and made a dignified exit, leaving Mycroft alone.

'Oh, dear,' he sighed to himself. 'Oh, dear.'

Fifteen

Dr Watson's Journal

Holmes returned just as the lamps were being lit along Baker Street, sending their pale amber beams into the growing evening gloom. Sitting at his chemical bench, a small mirror before him, my friend removed his disguise with speed and efficiency, flinging his false whiskers down with disdain.

'Argh,' he cried, 'spirit gum and horse hair are an excellent combination for irritating the skin. My chin feels like a raw piece of meat. Pour me a brandy, there's a good fellow. After tramping the streets of Shoreditch for most of the day, I need reviving.'

I did as requested and handed my friend his drink. 'Have your investigations borne fruit?' I asked, sitting opposite him by the fire.

'I'm not altogether sure. The proof will be in tonight's pudding. Suffice it to say, I have familiarised myself with every dismal nook and dark cranny of the Christopher Docks. There's not a potential hidey hole that I am not aware of.'

'How do you think they will strike?'

'My guess is that there will be a group of them. In the role of a pack of rowdy sailors they will attack the gentleman toff who has had the temerity to enter their territory. Anonymous they will emerge from the darkness and anonymous they will retreat into it.'

'And how on earth do you intend to foil such an attack?'

Holmes flashed me one of his infuriating smiles. 'You will have to wait and see.'

'But if you do not confide in me, how can I help you? Besides, by not revealing your plans you place my life in danger also.'

'Would I do such a thing, willingly? No, no, Watson, you will be at a safe distance, but you must carry your pistol and be ready to use it should the occasion demand it.' He drained his glass and rose briskly from the chair. 'Now I need to get out of these clothes, have a thorough wash, and relieve myself of the last vestiges of this gum. In the meantime would you be kind enough to rally Mrs Hudson to provide us with an early supper. A cold pie and meats will suffice. Some hearty vittles will set us both up for the rigours of this night. It is likely to prove both exerting and dangerous.' With these words, he retired to his room.

Just before ten o'clock that evening we left our chambers for another night-time adventure. Big Ben was chiming the hour as we hailed a cab. The sombre tones of the great bell booming solemnly on the cool night air seemed to match my mood. I was used to Holmes playing his cards close to his chest, failing to reveal to me the details of his plans. Indeed, I have lost count of the times we have ventured forth from Baker Street on a dangerous mission and I had no idea exactly what to expect. Of course, I trusted my friend implicitly and knew that he would not recklessly place my life or indeed his own in unnecessary danger, but, nonetheless, it was frustrating to be kept in the dark. I could not shrug off the feeling of dark apprehension about this night's activities.

On Holmes's instruction, I followed his example and had dressed down. While not quite in disguise, I had worn my oldest suit and a shabby overcoat which I had owned before I served in Afghanistan and had long intended to dispose of. Dressed in this manner, it was hoped that I would not draw attention to myself in the area of the city we were about to visit.

Some thirty minutes later, we alighted from our cab several streets away from the Christopher Docks in a narrow rubbish-strewn thoroughfare lined by a row of down-at-heel houses.

'Charming area, is it not?' said Holmes, casting a glance at the shabby domiciles. 'The Lord Nelson public house is two streets away, parallel to this one. When we arrive, I will enter on my own and you will come in several minutes later. On no account must you acknowledge that you know me.'

'I understand.'

'No doubt I will be approached and asked to accompany my contact to some dark and dismal place where they intend to dispose of me.' He gave a dry chuckle. 'Not such a long face, old fellow. Trust me. This evening is well orchestrated on my part. Attend to your duties and all will be well.'

'My duties. What are my duties?' I could not keep the note of irritation out of my voice.

'Follow me when I leave the Lord Nelson, making sure to keep a safe distance. You must not be seen. I will be taken to a meeting place where there will be a fracas. I can promise you that. During this melee, one or more of my attackers, most likely my contact, realising the game is up, will flee. It is your job to follow him. It is quite possible he will lead you to the gang's headquarters.' Holmes moved closer and grasped my arms. 'You are merely to note the location and return to Baker Street. On no account must you investigate further. It is not yet the time for heroics. Is that understood?'

I nodded my head.

'Don't look so glum. All will be well.'

Despite Holmes's confident manner, I was not at all sanguine about this risky affair. I had a nagging premonition that all would not go our way this night.

I waited five minutes after Holmes had disappeared inside the ale house before entering. The Lord Nelson was a noisy smoke-filled tavern filled with a crowd of rough-looking individuals, mainly men, loudly carousing and attempting, by the consumption of alcohol, to place the harsh realities of life at a distance. The few women present were middle aged or older and sat by themselves, solitary characters, apparently lost in thought while they nursed their glass of gin.

Despite my shabby attire, my appearance attracted some interest at first. I heard someone mutter, 'Ooh look, another toff,' and a few heads turned in my direction. But the novelty of my presence soon dissipated. I ordered a drink and sat at a table near the door.

Holmes was leaning on the bar, smoking a cigarette in a casual fashion and gave no indication that he had seen me. After some ten minutes, a scruffy bewhiskered individual with a patch over one eye, wearing a long, shabby soldier's greatcoat – one that had not seen a barracks in many a long year – approached him with a swagger. Leaning forward towards my friend he whispered something in his ear. Holmes nodded and flashed me the briefest of glances.

The one-eyed man gave some further gruff utterance, turned on his heel and headed for the door at a brisk pace. Holmes gave me a sly wink and followed him. Giving them less than a minute, I drained my glass, rose from my chair and made for the door. As I did so, a burly fellow in a rough tweed suit barred my way. 'Now where the hell d'you think you're going?' he demanded in a thick Irish brogue.

'What business is it of yours?' I asked.

'Hear that, boys? The fellow wants to know what business it is of mine–'

He got no further for I had delivered a heavy blow to the fellow's chin. The force of it and its surprise element so caught him off guard that he dropped like a felled tree. There was a mixture of laughter and angry uproar. A couple of men with knitted brows and clenched fists moved in my direction. It was clear that these were my assailant's confederates. With as much speed as I could muster, I stepped over the man's prone body and rushed out into the night.

In the distance I saw the silhouetted figures of Holmes and his companion, just before they turned left into another thoroughfare. I ran some way in their wake and then dived into a doorway just as three bruisers emerged noisily from the Lord Nelson in pursuit of me. Puzzled by the empty street before them, I could hear them discussing what to do next. Eventually, two of them hared off in the opposite direction, while the brute who had confronted me made his way with some haste up the street. I pulled back, deep into the shadows of the doorway. Without a glance my way, he passed me by.

Clasping the barrel of my revolver, I slipped out of my hiding place and, keeping to the shadows, followed the man. I soon caught up without the fellow being aware that I was on his tail. Stealthily, I crept up behind him, but just as I raised my gun to bring the butt down hard upon his skull, he faltered, sensing my approach. With an inarticulate grunt, he began to turn, but thankfully I was too quick for him. The metal connected with the back of his head. The brute uttered a guttural moan, his body shaking as if from the palsy, before he collapsed senseless onto the cobbles.

I tested his pulse. It was weak but regular. He would live, but have both an unpleasant wound and a severe headache for some time when he regained consciousness.

I wasted no more time on the fellow and recommenced my pursuit, hoping to catch up with Holmes and his guide before I lost them in the labyrinthine streets that lay beyond.

Luck certainly was on my side. I turned to the left, as I had seen Holmes and the other man do, and caught a sight of two shadowy figures in the distance. We were very near the Christopher Docks now, but I assumed that Holmes was being led to a location close by rather than to the docks themselves, to a secret lair for his assignation. I had no real idea what to expect, but I was determined to carry out my friend's orders.

Keeping close to the buildings, I moved swiftly and silently down the street. My quarry turned left through a gateway into the yard of a warehouse. On reaching it, I peered around the edge of the open rusted iron gates and saw Holmes and the rough standing facing each other in hushed conversation. The man in the greatcoat lit a cigarette, the match briefly illuminating his weathered features. This seemed to be some kind of signal for within seconds I observed six figures emerging from the shadows. Although their faces were indistinct, it was clear from their postures that their intentions were far from benevolent.

It was the ambush that Holmes had predicted, but now strangely he seemed to be unprepared. He stood casually, his body relaxed, apparently unaware of the threatening forms. I yanked my revolver from my pocket ready to fire at the men. I was about to call out to Holmes as a warning when, with amazing speed and dexterity, he pulled a silver whistle from the folds of his coat and gave three strong blasts on it.

The initial effect that this action had on the group advancing on him was one of confusion. They seemed disorientated and bewildered by this strange turn of events. Their discomfort grew all the more when suddenly from nowhere it seemed there was an army of other figures materialising out of the night. At least a dozen, I thought, moving swiftly. As they flashed across my vision, heading, as it turned out, to do battle with Holmes's enemies, I saw that they were raw youngsters, ill clad but agile and carrying sticks and iron bars. I recognised some of their faces. They were the Baker Street Irregulars.

Holmes must have arranged all this in advance. He had discovered through his investigations that the man would lead him here into this warehouse yard and that it would be a trap – a fatal trap. It was clearly intended that Holmes would not escape this encounter alive. I was both impressed and delighted at his perspicacity while at the same time dismayed, as usual, not to have been informed of his plans.

I had little time to contemplate either thought in detail as a dramatic skirmish played out before me. The Irregulars roared like savages as they approached the men who had been advancing on Holmes. It was with great pleasure that I saw them freeze with shock as the Irregulars set about them. It very quickly became evident that not only were the ruffians outnumbered by Holmes's troops, but they were also outclassed. The youngsters, nimble and better armed than their opponents, soon had the roughs beating a retreat. Two had fallen unconscious with bloody wounds to the head, while the others tried to escape, but to no avail. One lively youth jumped on the back of one of the men and beat him about the head with a stick until he crumpled to the floor unconscious.

I observed the man who had led Holmes to this spot slowly begin to edge his way backwards into the shadows, while the detective himself stood motionless, like an anthracite statue overseeing the proceedings. I was aware that it was my friend's intention to allow this scoundrel to escape and I knew that it was my job to follow him. On surveying the scene, I could see that none of the others would escape from the clutches of the Irregulars, but these felons were probably hired hands anyway and would have no real knowledge of the controlling power in this nefarious organisation. Holmes's companion, on the other hand, was a different kettle of fish. The one-eyed man skirted the warehouse walls and edged his way through the gates and out into the street. I was on his trail straight away.

My experiences with Holmes over the years have helped me to develop the stealthy talent for following a man without his knowledge. Crouching low, I peered around the gate and saw my quarry glancing back in my direction, making sure that he had slipped the net without hindrance. Then he hurried down the street at full pelt. After a moment's pause, I followed. As I travelled the dark streets in pursuit of the one-eyed man, I had little notion where this enterprise was going to lead me or how dangerous the outcome would be.

Sixteen

Sherlock Holmes was feeling rather pleased with himself as he sat back in his chair close to the dying embers of the fire in the sitting room of 221B Baker Street. He had treated himself to one of the cigars he kept in the coal scuttle and as he smoked it, he smiled. All had gone well tonight. Very well, indeed. The Irregulars had behaved magnificently, like a well-oiled machine, and the outcome of the skirmish was as he had planned it. The one-eyed man was obviously a lieutenant in the organisation and he would help to lead him, through Watson, to the centre of the web. The thought of this image brought to mind the late Professor James Moriarty. He had always regarded the professor as a cunning spider sitting at the centre of a giant web which had a thousand radiations. And Moriarty would know every quiver of each of them. The Temple kidnapping was an enterprise such as he would have masterminded. Holmes almost felt a twinge of regret that the criminal genius was no more, his bones beneath the turbulent waters of the Reichenbach Falls. However, it was clear that whoever this new nemesis was, he was from the same mould as the late-lamented professor.

Holmes glanced at his pocket watch. It was nearly three o'clock in the morning. He wondered how long it would be before Watson returned. He had seen him with wonderful stealth slip from the warehouse yard on the heels of the one-eyed man and he knew he could rely on his old friend to carry out his duties with aplomb. There was no man more worth having at your side when danger threatened than John Watson. With this thought in mind, Holmes puffed contentedly on his cigar.

The detective's confidence gradually began to fade as fingers of morning light reached in through the gaps in the blinds. He consulted his watch. Great heavens, it was nearly eight o'clock. Where on earth was Watson? Surely it could not have taken him all this time to follow the one-eyed man to his lair, note its location and return to Baker Street. Supreme logician though Holmes was, for a moment his mind avoided the obvious, the most probable reason for his friend's absence: that something had happened to him. Something unpleasant.

Holmes rose in an agitated fashion and began pacing the room. What on earth could he do? This was a situation he had not bargained for. Absentmindedly, he moved to the window and drew up the blinds, allowing the morning light to stream in. As he did so there was a knock at the door. For a moment his spirits rose, but then he sneered at his own foolishness: his friend never knocked at their own door. The knock came again. This time Holmes recognised the rhythm. It was Mrs Hudson.

'What time would you like breakfast, Mr Holmes?' she asked.

Holmes shook his head distractedly. 'I shall not require any today, thank you.'

'And Doctor Watson?'

'Watson… is out.'

'Oh, very well.' She could clearly tell Holmes was in one of his queer humours and so without further converse, she left the room.

With a weary shrug, Holmes retired to his bedroom where he shaved, changed into fresh clothes and tried to decide what his next course of action was going to be. When he returned to the sitting room, he immediately sensed another presence. At first he smiled, thinking that Watson had returned, but a gentle aroma of snuff soon informed him otherwise. Holmes's smile faded. Sitting, hidden from view in the winged armchair, was his brother, Mycroft.

'Good morning, Sherlock.'

'Mycroft,' Holmes responded. 'I am always fearfully disconcerted when I find you in the flesh in my chambers. I fear some catastrophe has taken hold of the country in order for you to make a detour from your fixed route between the government buildings and the Diogenes Club in order to visit me. Nothing pleasant would persuade you to alter your routine. So it must be doom and gloom.'

Mycroft gave the bleakest of smiles. 'As a consulting detective, doom and gloom are your veritable bread and butter.'

Holmes sat down across from his brother.

'I took the liberty of ordering coffee from Mrs Hudson on my way up. I am used to a warm libation at this time of the morning.'

As though on cue, there was a tap at the door, and the landlady entered with a tray bearing a coffee pot, milk jug and crockery.

'Would you like me to pour, gentlemen?' she asked.

'No, no, Mrs Hudson,' said Mycroft sweetly. 'We'll see to ourselves. Thank you so very much. I will let Sherlock be mother.'

After Mrs Hudson's swift departure, Holmes served the coffee with good grace.

'Thank you, Sherlock,' said Mycroft cheerily. 'No Watson, I see. Not back in practice or out ministering to some medical emergency for I observe his medical bag by the door.'

'What is the reason for this visit?' asked Holmes bluntly, resuming his seat.

'I think that you know very well why I'm here.'

'You've not had a ransom note yet or any kind of ultimatum.'

For the first time, Mycroft's features darkened and his brows furrowed into deep lines. He shook his head. 'No, we have not.'

'They are playing a long game.'

'Making us squirm, more like it.'

'Who are they?'

'I was hoping that you could tell me that.'

'Would I?'

'If you know, I would strongly advise it, Sherlock. I have no wish to see my brother carted off to the Tower of London.'

'As it happens I do not know. But you could do worse than take Mrs Chandler into custody.'

Mycroft's features softened once more and his lips parted in a thin smile. 'Would that we could. She and her assistant rats have fled the ship, I am afraid. We sent a posse round to her establishment yesterday to find the place deserted. No staff, no babies, no clues.'

'They are efficient, aren't they?'

'What do you know, Sherlock? It is imperative that you tell me and keep us informed of your investigations.'

'By "us" I suppose you refer to the British government.'

Mycroft did not reply.

Holmes sat back in his chair and steepled his fingers. 'To begin with I think it is essential that *you* present *me* with all the details of this dark scenario if only to confirm what I believe I already know.'

'I am sure that you do already know.'

'Indulge me.'

Mycroft heaved a sigh and took a sip of coffee, and then glowered at his brother over the rim of his cup. 'Very well,' he said at length. 'Some eight years ago, Prince Albert Edward, the Duke of Clarence, unwisely formed an attachment with a prostitute, Mary Kelly. So obsessed was he by this woman that he actually married her and indeed fathered a child by her. When this news reached certain individuals at the palace – do not ask me for their names for I cannot and indeed will not reveal them – plans were set in motion to destroy this unfortunate union... to do away with the mother and child. They were seen as a threat to the monarchy and the stability of government.'

Mycroft paused, expecting his brother to comment, but Holmes said nothing, his gaunt features set in a cold hard mask, his eyes glittering with disdain.

'And so the woman was sought out...'

'And slaughtered,' snapped Holmes with vehemence. 'Along with the others. All those in the know on the streets of Whitechapel fell victim to the Ripper, killer by royal appointment.'

Mycroft's hand flew up in alarm. 'You know that is not true. Her Majesty and her closest advisors, including the Prime Minister, had no knowledge of this.'

'But some people who could wield power did.'

Mycroft nodded. 'Matters got out of hand, it is true.'

Holmes gave a bitter laugh. 'You are a master of the diplomatic euphemism.'

'It is part of my trade and it is both a burden and a boon. But, to continue... Mary Kelly was killed, but the child was never found.'

'Until now.'

'Yes. The boy, effectively the heir to the throne, has been taken by persons unknown for reasons also as yet unknown.'

'But one can hazard a guess.'

'I believed that you never guess.'

'Don't let's play semantics, Mycroft. You know as well as I do that these malefactors are going to use the boy as a pawn, a lever to get what they want.'

'Oh, I agree. That is taken for granted. But what exactly do they want? That is the unanswered question. However, we cannot sit around doing nothing while we wait for this to become apparent. We have to act. *You* have to act.'

'Me?'

'You are already involved in the case. Now, you are being commanded—'

'Commanded?'

'Requested, if you prefer, by the Prime Minister to focus all your efforts in investigating this affair. It is of vital national importance.'

Holmes did not reply. He rose casually and retrieved his long grey pipe from the mantelpiece and filled the bowl with a quantity of shag from the Persian slipper in the hearth. Picking up the tongs he retrieved a cinder from the fire and carefully lit his pipe. When his features emerged from a cloud of pungent smoke, he spoke again.

'I am cognisant of the fact,' he said, 'that you have been placed in a difficult position. Ordered by your exalted masters to engage my services at all costs. You are not comfortable in the role, particularly as you know how stubborn and obtuse your brother can be.'

'Oh, yes, I am familiar with your intransigence.'

Holmes laughed. 'However, on this occasion, I accede to your request, but only on my terms.'

'I was fully expecting such a scenario.'

'Of course you were, brother mine. We can read each other's thoughts as easily as the agony column of *The Times*.'

'I never read the agony column of *The Times*, but I accept your analogy. What are your terms?'

'That I may carry out my investigations in my own fashion without help or hindrance from outside forces. I am an independent investigator, not a member of the constabulary. I must not be put under surveillance or shadowed in any way. You know I will soon very easily detect such a procedure. I will not report back each move I make or each shadow I see. I will only get in touch when a climax is about to be reached. You must wait for me to contact you. Is that understood and agreed?'

Mycroft opened his mouth to say something and then his eyes flickered with uncertainty. He closed his mouth and nodded his head. 'If it has to be this way…' he said at length.

'It does.'

'Very well. I will inform the Prime Minister. But, Sherlock, I need hardly state that this must be dealt with swiftly. Time is of the essence.'

'Indeed, you had no need to state that.'

Mycroft rose from his chair. 'I will leave you now, Sherlock. You have work to do.'

Holmes blew another cloud of smoke from his pipe, obscuring his face once again. 'Indeed.'

As Mycroft moved towards the door, he touched his brother's arm. 'Take care,' he said gently and then exited swiftly.

Holmes slumped down into his chair. Despite the dramatic implications of Mycroft's visit and the task before him, there was only one thought in the detective's mind: where on earth was Watson?

Seventeen

Dr Watson's Journal

I followed the one-eyed man through a maze of back streets, over walls and up narrow alleys. More than once I thought that I had lost him, but luck and my dogged tenacity kept me with him. At last he reached an alley near the Woolwich Road and approached a carriage that appeared to be waiting for him. Throwing his cap down in the gutter, he climbed into the carriage. It was at this point I thought I had lost the game. I was not expecting this development at all. No doubt in a few moments the carriage would set off with the one-eyed man inside and I would lose him. The rest of the thoroughfare was deserted and my chances of finding a cab at this time of night and in this locality in order to give chase were infinitesimal.

It was while I was considering this knotty problem that I noticed that the carriage had no driver. As I edged nearer, I felt a presence in the shadows behind me and then a sharp prod of something hard in the small of my back.

'It's loaded,' said a gruff voice in my ear. 'Any sudden moves and I will pull the trigger. You'll be dead in an instant.'

My heart sank. After all my efforts I had been caught. Deep disappointment rather than fear at my predicament robbed me of speech and I was unable to respond to my captor. He jabbed me with the barrel of the pistol once more. 'Move towards the carriage. We're going to take you on a little ride.'

Reluctantly I obeyed and, as I did so, the carriage door opened and the occupant stepped out. He was still dressed in his decrepit soldier's greatcoat and old clothes, but he had removed the eye patch and what had obviously been false whiskers and a wig. The fellow had been in disguise! I now gazed at the clear youthful features, unsullied by false accoutrements, and saw a finely chiselled countenance with a pair of bright intelligent eyes.

He stepped forward and placed his hand on my shoulder. It seemed almost a friendly gesture, especially as it was accompanied by a broad smile, but the cold gleam in those keen eyes told a different story.

'Ah, so it is Watson we have in our net. I had been hoping for your erstwhile companion Holmes.' He wrinkled his nose in mild annoyance. 'Not the chief but his deputy then. That is a pity – but...' Here he removed his hand from my shoulder and tapped me gently on the cheek. '...I suppose you'll do. Get inside and make it sharpish.'

The fellow behind me jabbed me once more in the ribs with the pistol. I knew for the moment there was nothing I could do but obey their command. As I stepped inside the carriage I received a heavy blow to the head and I fell forward, my mind whirling into unconsciousness.

* * *

I was propelled back into the world in a sudden and harsh fashion: doused with ice-cold water, which dragged me fully awake in an instant. I shook my head fiercely, dislodging droplets of water and clearing my vision. I was in a dimly lighted room, strapped securely to a chair and standing before me was the man whom I had followed from the Lord Nelson disguised as an old soldier and another man whose dark saturnine features I recognised immediately; it was Inspector Dominic Gaunt of Scotland Yard. Initially and foolishly, for a split second my heart leapt with joy, for I believed that I had fallen into the hands of the law after all. My brain was still befuddled from the blow, but my senses very quickly righted themselves. I realised that being coshed and bound were signs enough that these men were villains.

'Welcome back, Doctor,' said Gaunt smoothly. 'I have to admit that you are something of a disappointment to us. We were fully expecting Mr Holmes himself to be sitting where you are now.'

'You, sir, are the worst kind of malefactor. A policeman who abuses his position.'

Gaunt laughed loudly. 'Oh, I'm a malefactor am I? Well, I suppose I am. But, you see, I have always been one. My career in the police force has always been a disguise, a means by which I was able to further my plans and feather my own nest.'

'Then you are more despicable than I thought.'

Gaunt beamed. 'Probably. Malefactor and despicable? You see, Henshaw, we are in the company of a literary fellow. Well, maybe, Doctor, I am those things and more besides, but I have to inform you that I have the upper hand and that you are in my power.'

'For the moment perhaps.'

Gaunt laughed again 'Not only a medic with literary leanings but also with an absurd touch of bravado. Well, let me bring you down a little, my friend, with some rather brutal home truths. I intend to kill you shortly and I am not sorry to say that I shall have no qualms about it. However, before that eventuality, I shall use you to lure your interfering friend Sherlock Holmes into my clutches and then the two of you can be happily united in death.'

Fury coursed through my body and I wrestled with my bindings to no avail. I knew words were futile in this situation and I was not about to hurl abuse or curses at the fiend for this would only amuse him further.

Gaunt turned to his companion. 'Relieve him of his watch and chain. Trinkets that we'll use as bait.'

The man called Henshaw approached me and retrieved my gold watch, one that had belonged to my brother, along with my watch chain and fob, which was in the form of a small silver shield bearing the insignia of the 5th Northumberland Fusiliers. He handed them to his confederate who placed them in his jacket pocket.

'We'll leave you now, Doctor,' said Gaunt, suavely. 'As you are no doubt aware, you are securely bound; the room will be locked so there is no point in trying to escape. The best thing you can do is sit quietly and contemplate your imminent demise.'

He grinned briefly and then turned on his heel and both men left the room, slamming the door behind them. Then I heard the key turn in the lock. I was left in silent semi-darkness. Of course, I tried to wriggle free of my bonds, but they had been secured by an expert. There was no give at all in the cord that held me. I only served to scrape the skin on my wrists the more I struggled.

My spirits sank. It appeared there was nothing I could do to escape the fate that they had ordained for me. For me and Sherlock Holmes.

Eighteen

Dawn was breaking as Gaunt approached the big house; its black turrets, stark against the lightening sky, were haloed by the rays of the rising sun. The carriage rattled up the driveway at great speed: the driver knew it was in his best interests to convey his passenger as swiftly as possible. With a crunch and slither of wheels the carriage slewed to a halt by the main entrance. Gaunt jumped out.

'See to the horse,' he cried to the driver. 'I shall wish to return in an hour. Be ready.'

'Yes, sir,' the man replied, touching his cap.

Gaunt hurried up the steps to the house and disappeared inside.

'Your master is expecting me,' Gaunt said gruffly, handing his hat and gloves to a liveried servant.

'Indeed. He awaits you in the drawing room.'

Without another word, Gaunt strode off down the hall. He was very familiar with the layout of this house, as well he should be: he was a frequent visitor.

A fire burned brightly in the drawing room, but the curtains were still drawn and the lighting was subdued, filling the chamber with strange shifting shadows. A tall, distinguished-looking man who had been seated by the fire rose at Gaunt's approach; his face broke into a welcoming smile.

'Dom. Lovely to see you. '

The two men embraced. 'I was just about to pour myself a drink. It is early, I know, but I expect you could do with one yourself after the journey and the night's business,' said the tall man.

Gaunt nodded and took a seat by the fire.

'At my age I take no heed of the time or occasion regarding my drinking habits. If I desire a brandy, I pour a brandy,' said the tall man lightly. 'So, tell me all.'

'There have been some inconveniences I'm afraid.'

'Explain. I must pass on all the details to make sure our master is in full possession of the facts. It is he who dictates what action we take.'

Gaunt nodded. 'I am afraid Holmes has slipped through our net.'

The man emitted an exasperated groan. 'That man… I was warned that we would have problems with him once he had taken an interest in our dealings. He is more dangerous to us than all Scotland Yard put together. Blast him to kingdom come.'

Gaunt smiled. 'We may be about to do just that. While we may not have ensnared the main irritant, we have been able to snatch his subservient partner.'

The tall man paused in his task of pouring the drinks and turned to his young companion, a look of mild puzzlement on his face. 'Subservient partner…? You mean that fellow Watson?'

'The same. Doctor John Watson, Holmes's companion,

biographer and close friend. We have him at Greenway. He will be used as bait to lure Mr Holmes into our clutches.'

'Well, let us hope so. That is encouraging. I will delay passing on the information regarding our little setback for the moment. It will only upset and anger him. Better we come with the news of Holmes's demise. As things stand now, it would be imprudent to make any move until we are sure that Holmes is out of the way – permanently. This operation is delicate enough without having to deal with his interference as well.'

The tall man handed Gaunt his drink. 'Thank you,' he said, taking a generous gulp. 'A day, two at the most, and I believe it will all be over. Holmes will be found floating in the Thames with his throat cut. And, let's face it, a few more days of silence will make the government all the more jittery.' He chuckled at the thought.

The tall man stroked his chin thoughtfully. 'I am relying on you, Dom. This matter is crucial.'

Gaunt leaned forward in his chair and touched the man's arm. 'I know,' he said quietly.

'Good. Would you like to see the child before you go?'

'Indeed, I would.'

'So you shall. I think it is time to take him further down the bumpy road he is travelling. Finish your drink first and then I'll take you to see him.'

Ten minutes later the tall man led Gaunt up into the upper reaches of the house. Down a narrow corridor, a stout middle-aged man was sitting guard outside a door, an oil lamp guttering on a small table beside him. On seeing them, the man rose automatically. 'Sir,' he said gruffly, in a manner that suggested that his voice was hardly ever used.

'All well, Taylor?' the tall man asked.

Taylor raised his hand to his forehead in a rough salute. 'Nothing to report, sir.'

The tall man nodded. 'Good. Open up.'

Thrusting back the flap of his jacket, Taylor retrieved a key which hung from his belt and used it to unlock the door. Gaunt and his companion entered the room beyond. It was a large chamber, dimly lighted, which contained a capacious bed, a wardrobe and a few chairs. On one of these sat the nurse, who in a similar manner to that of Taylor rose formally as the visitors entered. Sitting cross-legged on the bed was the young boy. He had a sketch pad across his knees and was drawing. He glanced up at the two men.

'Have you come to take me home?' he cried, disposing of the sketch pad in an instant and jumping off the bed.

'You have been told before that this is your home now. We are your new family,' said the tall man, not unkindly.

'No you're not. You are bad men. I hate you.'

'Now, now, Master William,' said the nurse, 'you don't mean that.'

'Yes, yes, I do. I want my mother.'

The tall man sighed. 'The woman who claimed to be your mother is dead. And so is the man who pretended to be your father.'

The boy froze in shock at these words, his face twisted with horror and disbelief. It was clear to Gaunt that his young mind was having difficulty in taking in the full implications of the dreadful news that the two people whom he had regarded as his parents were dead.

'No, no. It isn't true. You lie,' cried the boy, tears springing from his eyes. He launched himself at the tall man, beating him with his fists.

With ease, the man held the boy off. 'Now why would I lie? What possible reason could I have for making up such a story?'

Holding the boy by his shoulder, the tall man knelt down so that their faces were on a level.

'Look, William, I know how hard this is for you, but the sooner you accept the fact that you will never see those people again, the better it will be.'

The boy's face crumpled and he pulled away and threw himself back on the bed sobbing, his body shuddering. The nurse made a move to comfort him, but the tall man stopped her with an imperious gesture. 'No,' he said, shaking his head. 'He must learn to come to terms with this on his own. Sympathy and coddling will only delay the process. Don't you agree, Dom?'

Gaunt nodded. It was of no consequence. To him the boy was just a pawn in their game, dispensable when their object had been achieved.

'Time I was returning to the city. I have work to do at the Yard and a trap to set.'

The tall man smiled. 'God speed.'

Nineteen

Sherlock Holmes returned to Baker Street late that afternoon. He was in disguise once more as a rough sailor. He maintained the hunched shambling gait until he had closed the street door behind him and finally stood erect in the hallway and stretched, easing his body back into its natural shape and height. He didn't quite know what to make of his afternoon's expedition, but at least he had discovered a further thread in the mystery. And this had been purely by chance. He had spent some time scouring the streets around the Christopher Docks, even revisiting the Lord Nelson to see if he could catch sight of any of the men who had been involved in last night's operation – anything that might give him a lead as to where Watson was. His search had been fruitless, as he imagined it would be. He knew that he was grasping at straws. Those felons would be lying low today, especially after the outcome of the previous evening's debacle. Many would be slumped in their beds nursing their wounds and their pride.

Reluctantly, Holmes had come to the conclusion that Watson's absence meant only one thing: the villains had him in their clutches. They had failed in their main aim – getting rid of him – but had succeeded in capturing Watson. He prayed that indeed they were keeping him prisoner somewhere and had not done away with his friend. Waves of guilt crashed over Holmes as he contemplated that particular outcome. Never had he felt as helpless and impotent in an investigation and he was aware that because of Watson's involvement, he was allowing emotion to interfere with his judgement. Usually, no matter how dramatic or dangerous an investigation, he was able to remain clear-sighted and objective, dealing solely with facts and circumstances in a cold, precise manner. This was not the case now.

As he was about to ascend the seventeen steps up to his sitting room, Mrs Hudson emerged from her quarters. She was quite used to Holmes appearing in the hallway in all manner of disguises. She had a sharp feminine eye and unlike Watson was rarely fooled by the detective's theatrics.

'Oh, Mr Holmes,' she said matter-of-factly as she addressed the old sea dog, 'you have a visitor. He has been waiting for you some thirty minutes. A gentleman from Scotland Yard.'

Holmes nodded his thanks and as he made his way up the stairs, he removed much of the facial appendages of his disguise – whiskers, false nose and wig – stuffing them in the pocket of his pea jacket. On entering the sitting room he discovered Inspector Dominic Gaunt standing by the hearth perusing a small booklet. Holmes recognised it as one of his own monographs, which the inspector must have taken from the bookcase to browse while he waited for him.

Gaunt raised a surprised eyebrow at the detective's appearance.

Despite removing the elements of disguise that concealed his real features, Holmes still appeared out of character in his shabby, disreputable clothes and generally unkempt appearance.

'On a case, I see?' observed Gaunt wryly.

Holmes flung off his coat, ignoring the remark. 'What can I do for you, Inspector? I had not expected to see you again so soon.' His manner was brusque bordering only slightly on the side of civility.

Gaunt smiled gently. 'They have Watson,' he said simply.

Holmes froze and his eyes widened with surprise. 'How do you know?' He was genuinely puzzled and full of apprehension.

Gaunt reached into his inside pocket and retrieved a gold watch and chain with a fob with which Holmes was most familiar. 'This arrived at the Yard this lunchtime – addressed to you.'

Holmes held out his hand. Gaunt passed him the watch. Holmes inspected the timepiece carefully. It was Watson's without a doubt. 'It is strange that it was sent to Scotland Yard if it was meant for me,' he observed, cradling the watch in the palm of his hand. 'Why not have it delivered to Baker Street?'

Gaunt shrugged. 'Perhaps they wanted to let us know that they are one jump ahead of even the great Sherlock Holmes.' There was no sarcasm in Gaunt's tone, but the words certainly carried the feeling.

'They? And who do you suppose "they" are?'

'The villains who kidnapped the boy. As to their identities your guess is as good as mine.'

'I do not guess,' said Holmes tartly. 'Was there a note, some communication with the watch?'

Gaunt nodded. He extracted a sheet of paper from his coat and handed it to Holmes, who took it and moved to the window, retrieving his magnifying glass from the chemical bench. Holding the paper to the light, he scrutinised it carefully. He said nothing but made gentle murmurs as the glass moved over the contents. There was a message printed in capital letters. It read:

DEAR SHERLOCK

WE HOLD DR WATSON PRISONER AND HIS LIFE IS AT RISK UNLESS YOU DO AS WE TELL YOU. IF YOU WANT TO SEE HIM AGAIN BE ON WATERLOO BRIDGE TONIGHT AT MIDNIGHT. COME ALONE. DO NOT TRY TO BE CLEVER. ONE MISTAKE ON YOUR PART AND WATSON'S THROAT WILL BE CUT.

'What do you make of it?' asked Gaunt.

'Very little,' replied the detective guardedly. 'It has the tone of a penny dreadful, but the message is clear enough.'

'Surely you will not attend the rendezvous?'

Holmes said nothing, but raised his eyebrows.

'It would be madness.'

'I shall have to. I have been given no alternative.'

'We can have a body of men standing by…'

'No!' cried Holmes. 'I must adhere to their instructions. I must go there alone.'

'Your life will be in danger.'

'Of course, but if I do not, they will kill Watson. I cannot allow that. But I must impress upon you that the police must not be involved in this venture. Is that understood?'

Gaunt hesitated, his brow creased in consternation. 'If you so wish it.'

'I command it.'

'I do not know what my superiors will have to say about this. I cannot see them allowing you to face these villains alone.'

'If your superiors or indeed you have any concerns over this matter, you should consult my brother, Mycroft, who is acting for the Prime Minister in this matter. I am sure he will confirm that my wishes must be adhered to.'

Gaunt pursed his lips before replying. 'Very well,' he said. 'All there remains for me to do is wish you good luck.'

'I thank you for your sentiments, Inspector, but I fear that luck will play little part in tonight's adventure.'

Gaunt made a move to leave, but Holmes stepped forward to halt his progress. 'Tell me, Inspector,' he said, 'how were the watch and the note delivered to Scotland Yard?'

Gaunt seemed somewhat nonplussed by this question and it took him a few moments to reply. 'They were handed in at the main desk in a brown paper parcel. It was addressed to you, but landed up on my desk because… they knew I'd been to see you recently concerning the kidnapping case.'

'I see. Do you have the wrapping paper from the parcel?'

'Well, no. I discarded it once the contents had been revealed.'

Holmes sighed. 'That was most injudicious. It may have told us many things.'

'It was just two sheets of brown paper…'

'With writing upon it?'

'Yes. But quite insignificant.'

'It is often the insignificant that can lead one to the significant.'

Gaunt looked blankly at the detective.

Holmes sighed again and then allowed himself a bleak smile. 'Never mind,' he said. 'At least we have the note. I trust you have no objection to me keeping this for the moment. A further study of it may provide some clues as to the author.'

'Of course.' Gaunt moved to the door, retrieving his hat from the rack. 'Now, Mr Holmes,' he said, turning to face the detective again, 'are you absolutely certain that you would not like some police assistance tonight? I fear for your safety and feel somewhat guilty at letting you tackle this matter on your own.'

'Your conscience can be clear. I absolve you of all responsibility in this matter. I am convinced that it is imperative that I make this assignation on my own.'

'Very well. Good day, Mr Holmes.'

'Inspector.'

As soon as the door had closed, Holmes emitted one of his high-pitched chuckles. 'The nerve of the man,' he said to himself, throwing off his seaman's coat. Still smiling he dashed into his bedroom, emerging in less than a minute, sober-suited and pulling on his overcoat. He raced down the stairs and was out on the street just in time to see the figure of Inspector Gaunt some hundred yards ahead of him. Luckily dusk had fallen now and pedestrians were merging into the evening shadows. Fortunately for Holmes, Gaunt made an imposing figure with his height and top hat and he was easy to keep in view from a distance.

'Now, where are you going to, my fine fellow?' murmured Holmes to himself as he set forth in swift pursuit.

As he stalked his prey in a brisk fashion, he turned over in his mind the points of interest that had prompted him to shadow the Scotland Yard man. For a start there was the rather vague account of how the package containing Watson's watch had come into his possession. Very strange that an inspector of Gaunt's standing had not felt it important to retain the wrapping and bring it with him. Maybe that was because there was no wrapping. Similarly, why on earth should the villains send the watch there rather than to him personally at Baker Street? Holmes thought he knew why. Then there was the paper on which the note had been written. Although it had no visible water mark, he recognised it easily as standard Metropolitan Police issue: the sort found in all offices at the Yard. Its flimsy coarseness and ivory tinge were familiar to him, as was the murky brown ink, which was typical of the type used in that establishment. He recognised these aspects from the many notes sent to him by Lestrade and Gregson in the past. So it was clear to him that the whole scenario concerning the package was false. Holmes reasoned that there could only be one sensible explanation for such a deception: Gaunt had come into possession of the watch by other means and he had concocted this fairy tale to disguise the fact. Holmes knew that the watch was a family heirloom, having belonged to Watson's brother and therefore had great sentimental value to his friend. Watson carried it with him wherever he went. The only way Gaunt could have got hold of the watch was by taking it from its owner.

If all these deductions were accurate – and Holmes did not doubt they were – then it pointed to one terrible fact. Inspector Dominic Gaunt was in league with the kidnappers. This being the case, Holmes wondered if Gaunt was just a rogue operative or part of a covert organisation within the establishment. Was he once more at odds with those in power as he had been in the days of the Ripper?

At the corner of Baker Street, Gaunt paused and for a moment seemed uncertain what to do. Holmes slipped into the gutter behind a stationary wagon loaded with barrels. Peering around the side, he was able to observe Gaunt. After lighting a cigarette, the inspector stepped into the road to hail a cab. Holmes moved swiftly, keeping to the shadows until he was within eight feet of his quarry. He knew that he was taking a risk coming so close, but he was determined to hear the instructions given to the cabby. Gaunt was too intent on flagging down a cab to notice the lean figure hovering in the darkness.

A hansom pulled up and Gaunt flung the door open. 'Prince's Square, Bayswater,' he cried before disappearing inside.

Holmes allowed himself a brief smile and then waited only a few seconds before attempting to secure a cab for himself. In such a busy thoroughfare there were always plenty of such conveyances.

Holmes brandished a sovereign at the driver and pointed to Gaunt's cab, now some hundred yards ahead of them and already merging into the throng of vehicles.

'Keep that hansom in view if you can,' Holmes cried. 'They are heading for Prince's Square in Bayswater. There's another sovereign for you if you don't lose them.'

'Right you are,' returned the driver, whipping up his steed.

The street was thick with traffic and progress was slow, but Holmes's driver was an adept fellow and by careful and clever weaving between the various carts and carriages in his path he was able to draw closer to the other hansom. Once out of the thick congestion of the West End, the going was much easier and both cabs were able to speed up. However, while keeping a measured distance Holmes's driver never lost sight of his quarry.

After some thirty minutes, they had reached Bayswater. 'Prince's Square is the next on the left, sir,' cried the driver.

'Good man,' said Holmes, swinging the door open and leaning out. 'Pull up here. This will do me admirably.'

Slipping the cabby a further sovereign, Holmes darted down the street in the wake of Gaunt's cab. He had almost caught up with it when it turned left into Prince's Square. It was a neat and smart oasis with a small but tidy railed garden area in the centre surrounded on all four sides by rows of elegant Georgian houses.

The driver drew up outside one of the more imposing edifices. After his cab had departed, Gaunt mounted the steps and rang the bell. Holmes slipped into the park area and hid behind a tree with a clear vantage point to observe events. In due course the door of the house opened, but only enough for the person on the inside to observe who the visitor was. This individual was shrouded in shadow and Holmes could not even tell if it was a man or a woman. A few words were exchanged and then Gaunt entered, the door slamming shut behind him.

Holmes studied the building. A plaque on the gatepost announced it as 'Greenway'. It was a three-storey Georgian villa, tall and slender like its neighbours, but all the curtains and blinds were drawn as though the property was shut up. It stood in the gloom like a ghost house. It was a house that harboured dark secrets and Sherlock Holmes knew it was his task to uncover them.

Twenty

Gaunt and Henshaw sat in the large empty kitchen of the house in Prince's Square and drank whisky while the inspector gave him details of his meeting with Sherlock Holmes. The room was illuminated by candlelight only, and a meagre fire glowed feebly in the grate.

Henshaw grinned and ran his fingers through the thick unruly thatch of blonde hair, but Gaunt was not smiling.

'Don't think for one minute that Holmes was fooled by the watch and my story. He is far too clever for that. I could see the suspicion in his eyes. We made the mistake of underestimating him last night; we must not do the same again.'

Henshaw's grin faltered. 'What is your plan then? Do I need to round up the boys again?'

Gaunt shook his head. 'And have a repeat performance of the Christopher Docks shambles? No. Tonight there will be no mass ambush. Tonight I will kill Mr Sherlock Holmes myself.'

Henshaw's eyes widened in surprise. 'And how do you

intend to do that?' he asked nervously.

Gaunt was pleased at the effect his statement had made on his companion and he smiled. 'I shall shoot him. No matter how many of his young cronies he assembles as a backup, the man himself will be a sitting duck on Waterloo Bridge. And I am a crack shot with a rifle.' Gaunt raised an imaginary weapon to his shoulder and aimed at the far distance. 'Bang! One bullet and it's goodbye, old Sherlock.'

Henshaw chuckled. 'Very nice.'

Gaunt drained his glass. 'But first, I think it's time we delivered the other member of this interfering partnership into the hands of his maker. Doctor Watson is of no use to us now. It will give me great pleasure to put him out of his misery. If you would be so kind as to lend me your pistol.'

'Of course.' Henshaw retrieved a small gun from the inside pocket of his greatcoat and handed it to Gaunt.

Gaunt fondled it for a moment and then stood up quickly, pushing the wooden chair back on the flagstones, creating a strange high-pitched squeaking sound that echoed around the chamber. 'Come on, Henshaw, let's get the job over with. It's time we had a little fun.'

Without further words the two men made their way up to the top storey of the house and the locked room where they had imprisoned Watson.

Henshaw retrieved the large key that was attached to his belt, opened the door and stepped into the room. He turned up the gas, filling the room with a rich yellow glow. Watson raised his head and gazed groggily at the intruders.

'Time to meet your maker now, old boy,' said Gaunt, holding the pistol aloft.

'I think not,' said a voice behind him, and Gaunt felt the cold sensation of a gun barrel pressed hard into the nape of his neck.

'Drop your weapon,' said the voice. Gaunt recognised it in an instant. It belonged to Sherlock Holmes. He lowered his arm, but still retained his hold on the gun.

'Do as I say,' came the voice again and Gaunt heard the sharp click as Holmes cocked the pistol. Reluctantly, Gaunt allowed his gun to drop from his grasp. It hit the floor with a dull thud.

'You,' snapped Holmes, addressing Henshaw, who seemed held in a trance, frozen by shock. 'Untie your prisoner. Do it now and do it quickly.'

Like an automaton, Henshaw shuffled over to where Watson was bound and began to loosen his bonds in a slow mechanical fashion. While this was happening, Gaunt took a chance and made a desperate move. Quickly sidestepping to the left and spinning round, he attempted to knock the gun out of Holmes's hand. He failed, but the gun went off, the bullet thudding harmlessly into the wooden floorboards. This sudden distraction appeared to bring Henshaw to his senses and dropping to the ground he made a grab for Gaunt's discarded pistol. With lightning swiftness, Holmes stepped forward and kicked the gun, sending it skittering into the corner of the room before Henshaw could snatch it up.

By now Gaunt had slipped past Holmes and was out in the corridor. He slammed the door of the room shut and turned the key, locking it. With a sardonic grin, he raced down the stairs, making good his escape.

Inside the chamber, Henshaw had taken advantage of the distraction caused by Gaunt's exit and had scrabbled across the floor to retrieve the gun. With a cry of satisfaction he grabbed it and, clambering to his feet, aimed it at Holmes. Without hesitation, he pulled the trigger. The detective feinted to the left, the bullet just clipping the shoulder of his overcoat. Henshaw roared his dismay and was about shoot again, but Holmes fired first. Henshaw was hit in the chest and the force of the blow flung his body backwards. With an animal-like bellow he crashed against the far wall of the room, and then slowly slithered down to the floor, leaving a thin crimson trail of blood in his wake.

For a moment, everything was silent and still. Holmes gazed down at the dead man whose lifeless glassy eyes seemed to stare back at him with vehemence. Holmes hated killing, but was particularly annoyed that it had been necessary in this instance. This man, Gaunt's accomplice, could have told him so much. With the thought of Gaunt, Holmes's features tightened even more with anger and disgust. Not only had he killed an important witness, but he had allowed one of the key players in this treacherous game to escape. He had handled the whole episode incompetently.

His thoughts were interrupted by a soft groaning sound and he observed a desperate Watson, trying manfully to wriggle his way out of his bonds.

Holmes could not help but smile. *Well,* he mused, *this episode is not entirely without its rewards.*

'Here, let me help you with those,' he said, kneeling down by the chair and tackling one of the tightest knots.

Twenty-One

Dr Watson's Journal

It was all like a bad dream. The gunshots and the frantic action being played out before my dazed eyes like some violent mummer's play in shimmering gaslight. I was tired, weak from exhaustion and dehydrated and so my brain was not functioning clearly. However, the one thing that I was able to latch on to was that Sherlock Holmes was in the room. How he got there and even why he was there did not seem to trouble or intrigue me, so foggy was my mind. I just felt a strange kind of relief to see his face and hear his voice. I remember him kneeling beside me, untying the rope that secured me to the chair and I have recollections of him helping me down various flights of stairs and then the sharp cold of the night air on my face. It was hours later, when I regained consciousness fully, that my memory returned and I was able to place recent events into perspective. I was lying on the chaise longue in our sitting room, a travelling rug covering me up to my chin.

'Ah, you are back in the land of the living, at last. I'm sure you could manage some of Mrs Hudson's chicken soup. She has had it simmering in anticipation since she helped me upstairs with you.'

I sat up and ran my fingers through my hair. 'Soup would be wonderful. I would like a brandy to help revive me further, but perhaps not on an empty stomach.'

Holmes nodded. 'Indeed,' he said judiciously, lighting his pipe. 'That can come later.'

I attempted to swing my legs on to the ground and stand up, but I still felt a little woozy and slumped back down on the chaise longue.

'Sit still, old boy. Let the restorative soup have its way with you first before you start trying to be athletic. Just rest for now while I go and arrange for your sustenance.'

An hour later, I was beginning to feel more like my old self. The cobwebs in my brain and the fatigue in my limbs were fading and I was able to sit up with a cigarette and a glass of brandy. Holmes, puffing on his old cherrywood pipe, had recounted all that had happened during my enforced absence and I had related my miserable adventures in return.

'Despite all the drama,' I said, 'we do not seem to be much further along with this investigation.'

'Indeed, everything is tenuous. There is very little one can actually get hold of, to grasp to one's bosom as proof or progress. Certainly we have lifted the stone and found insects beneath. Gaunt has been exposed for the traitorous villain that he is.'

'It is such a pity that he managed to escape.'

'My incompetence, I am afraid. I should not have let it happen.'

'It was not your fault, Holmes,' I said briefly. I knew that his attention and concerns were for my safety and it was this focus that had allowed Gaunt to make his escape. I was aware that Holmes would not welcome me airing such thoughts and so I moved the conversation on.

'How on earth did you discover where I was being kept prisoner?'

'By simply following Gaunt. I never liked the man. When he first came to Baker Street, I saw that there was something arrogant and false about him. It was clear to me that he was lying about how your watch had come into his possession. He had obviously concocted the tale, saying a packet had been delivered but with no evidence of the wrapping. Then there was the note on Yard paper written with that iodine-coloured ink that Lestrade and his cronies use. There was something about his whole demeanour that was suspicious. That's why I followed him. He led me to the house, Greenway, where you were being kept. I observed the barred upper window and the flickering gaslight. An ideal location to secrete a prisoner.' Holmes laughed. 'I knew I was taking a risk, but I was prepared to do it. I made my way to the rear of the building and managed to shin up a drainpipe to the second floor. With care and as silently as I could I broke a pane of glass in the window on the landing and let myself into the house. I pulled the curtain across the window so that anyone passing inside the house would not see the damage. Then I heard voices coming up the stairs – Gaunt and his henchman. They mentioned your name and so I knew that indeed I was on the right track.'

'Are you any clearer as to what these people are after and why they have kidnapped the child?'

Holmes shrugged. 'Nothing is clear yet. Obviously they wish to have power over the government, maybe even the throne, but I am not sure what they want. It cannot be long before they reveal their demands. The only comforting fact in all this business is their determination to destroy me. They obviously see me as a threat and I suspect despite their failure in this department, they will now be making plans to bring this venture to a successful conclusion.'

'At least you have unmasked one of the gang: that devil Gaunt.'

Holmes nodded. 'His involvement in this matter reveals how wide these villains have spread their net: into Scotland Yard and possibly beyond. It alerts one to the fact that you should trust no one, no matter their status. Gaunt seems to have fooled even my brother.'

'Your brother? Mycroft?'

'Indeed. I have received orders from on high to solve this case. We have been retained by the British government.'

'Great heavens. The case grows in its enormity moment by moment. What is your next move?'

For a moment Holmes paused before replying, puffing on his pipe with such force that his features were shrouded in grey smoke. 'Follow up the trail left by Gaunt,' he said at length. 'I doubt if he has left us many – if any – clues in his wake, but perhaps he wasn't reckoning on such a sleuth-hound as myself to be so close on his tail. I need to examine his office at the Yard and his home, wherever that may be. We should be able to find something, one little something that will take us one or two steps further down the road to clearing up this murky business.'

And so it was very early the next morning, we found ourselves in the office of Detective Inspector Gaunt at Scotland Yard, accompanied by our old friend, Inspector Giles Lestrade. Holmes had told him a discreet and highly edited version of our involvement in the Temple kidnapping case, enough to satisfy his curiosity and allow him to be of use to us. After a good night's sleep and one of Mrs

Hudson's hearty breakfasts, I was feeling my old self again and content to be accompanying Holmes on the case once more.

'I never liked Gaunt, Mr Holmes,' Lestrade was saying as Holmes examined the contents of the wastepaper basket. 'He was too cocky by half. Typical of the new breed of inspectors they are training up. None of them seem to fully comprehend the nature of this job. You need to serve your time on the beat to get to know how a villain's mind works. Yes, never took to him, but I must say I am shocked to hear that he is a wrong 'un.'

'"Wrong 'un" aptly describes the fellow,' smiled Holmes, replacing the wastepaper basket. We watched as he opened each drawer of the desk and sifted meticulously through the contents. 'It is as I thought,' he murmured at one juncture, more to himself rather than to Lestrade or me. 'Gaunt has covered his tracks well. There is nothing here but trivial official papers and notes. Nothing relating to the Temple kidnapping in any way.'

Then Holmes encountered a locked drawer. He flashed a knowing look at me as he retrieved the letter opener from the desk and attacked the lock. After a short time, he was able to wrench the drawer open. Lestrade and I gathered round, as Holmes withdrew a cardboard file from within. He laid it on the desk and opened it out. Within were two photographs and what appeared to be a set of letters. One photograph was of William Temple, a cabinet portrait taken in a studio, as was the other photograph, which was of Mr and Mrs Temple. On the reverse of each of these photographs was the name of a photography studio, situated on the Strand.

'No doubt Gaunt had no difficulty obtaining these. They would be used to allow his kidnappers to familiarise themselves with their targets.'

'What about the letters, Mr Holmes?' asked Lestrade, leaning over the desk and peering at the sheets of paper.

Holmes did not reply immediately, but examined two of the missives in great detail.

'They are letters addressed to "Dear G" and signed "J".'

'G would be Gaunt,' said Lestrade.

'Well done, Lestrade. I think you have it,' said Holmes, allowing a brief smile to touch his lips. 'But can you tell me who "J" is?'

The policeman shook his head.

'Neither can I, but from the tone of the letters, he seems to be Gaunt's superior; the captain of the ship, if you will. Take this letter for instance.'

Holmes spread it out on the desk so that we could peruse it.

Dear G

All is in place. We are ready to receive the packet.
Suggest that it arrives on Tuesday after dusk.
Pay off the grotesques. We shall not require their services again.

I look forward to being in your company again.

J

'I assume that "the packet" refers to the boy, William,' I said.

'That is how I read it also.'

'What about "the grotesques"?' asked Lestrade.

Holmes frowned. 'From the tone of the document, the quality of the paper and the florid handwriting, I would deduce that the author is an educated man of some wealth and power. As such he would regard those who work for him in low esteem. I should say that the grotesques are hired hands who have been involved in this venture but are really of no great consequence. Maybe they were the actual kidnappers. Certainly the description of them given to us by Mrs Temple and her nurse clearly indicated that they were no beauties: grotesques, in fact.'

'The question remains as to where the package was delivered.'

'Quite so, Watson. Maybe we shall get further clues from the other letters. If you gentlemen will take a seat, I will study them to see what fresh information they present.'

We did as we were asked, or at least I took a chair by the door while Lestrade stood by the window gazing out over the rooftops as he fiddled absentmindedly with his watch chain.

Holmes was seated at the desk, his magnifying lens roving slowly over the letters. From time to time he uttered brief inarticulate noises, which gave no indication as to whether they were utterances of pleasure or disappointment.

At last, he stood up, slipping his lens back in his inner coat pocket. 'These letters do not tell us much, but they do tell us something.'

'What exactly?' asked Lestrade gruffly.

'The correspondent is a man of wealth, as I said. The paper is of highest quality and of a particular hue and so was no doubt a special order. It may be possible to trace him through stationers. My first port of call would be Woodall and Brough on Jermyn Street. The handwriting with its broad strokes and artistic curlicues suggests an extravagant and emotional nature. However, the tone is very much of one in control. The letters are peppered with phrases like "you must", "it is imperative that you" and "do not, under any circumstances". Nevertheless the writer is cunning enough never to refer to anything specifically, as with the reference to "the packet" when it no doubt referred to the abducted child.'

'Not a lot to go on there then,' sniffed the policeman, dismissively.

'Indeed, I said as much. There is one other point, however: in one of the letters he says that he is "looking forward to you coming down". "Coming down" is a phrase used by those who live out of London, in the country, which suggests this fellow has a house in the country.'

'Well, there are hundreds of those,' growled Lestrade.

Holmes pursed his lips, a gesture completely missed by the inspector.

'I will leave the letters here for you to study further, Lestrade,' said Holmes briskly. 'We have work to do elsewhere.'

'Do you wish for my assistance?'

'No, no. I think you might be better employed informing your superiors concerning Inspector Gaunt and trying to track him down. My inquiries will lead me elsewhere.'

'The fool!' cried Holmes sharply, as we settled back in the hansom cab after leaving Scotland Yard. We were on our way to Streatham to the home of Dominic Gaunt in search of further clues. 'Despite all the years we have been associated with Lestrade, he seems to have learned nothing about the subtleties of detective work. He wants his clues presented to him gift-wrapped. He seems incapable of realising that small indications can lead to large outcomes. There is nothing so important as trifles in an investigation.'

'You can lead a horse to water, eh, Holmes?'

My friend chuckled. 'That's one way of looking at it. No doubt the bird will have flown his coop and taken much evidence with him, but he will, by necessity, have had to act in haste. He knew we would be close on his heels. And in that haste he may well have been careless. We can but hope.'

Gaunt lived down a tidy little street of terraced houses, respectable without being grand. There was a small garden with a privet hedge leading to a porch and a brightly painted front door.

'I am afraid we shall have to become unlawful intruders once again,' Holmes announced glibly as he retrieved a small thin metal object from the inside pocket of his coat, which he applied to the lock on the front door. 'You know, Watson, if my predilections had not led me down the righteous path to solving crimes and misdemeanours, I think I could have made a healthy living as a thief.'

In less than a minute there was a satisfying click from the lock and Holmes was able to turn the handle and open the door. We made our way inside and into a sitting room. It was well-ordered and Spartan but the drawers of the desk in one corner and the cupboard doors of a sideboard in the other were both open, revealing that they were empty. Holmes knelt by the grate and gazed at the pile of ashes there. Slipping off his gloves, he dipped his fingers into them. 'Still warm. He made a little bonfire of any evidence that may have been of use to us.'

Methodically, we searched every room, but it was clear that Gaunt had done a thorough job of removing or destroying any clues. In his bedroom, his wardrobe was empty apart from a few shirts and one old suit: neither bore the maker's name.

Holmes sighed heavily. 'I think we have gleaned as much as we can here,' he observed gloomily, 'which is nothing.' He was about to leave the room when he stopped suddenly, his attention caught by an etching hanging on the wall. It was of a large manor house set in extensive grounds.

'That's strange,' he murmured, moving to take a closer look at the picture.

'What is strange?' I asked.

'Did you not notice that Gaunt had a similar drawing, maybe the same one, in his office at Scotland Yard?'

I confessed that I had not observed it.

'I wonder where this is. There is no title and the artist has not signed it. To have two pictures of the same house is most suggestive.'

'In what way?' I asked, unable to follow Holmes's train of thought.

'Well, the house must have some special significance for him to have a representation of it in both his place of work and at home. Remember that phrase from the letter: "coming down". Maybe this is the property that was indirectly referred to.'

'By Jove, yes, that may indeed be the case.' I nodded in agreement.

Holmes took the picture down from the wall and prised open the back of the frame to retrieve the print. 'Let's call this a promising souvenir,' he said, rolling up the drawing and slipping it into his inside pocket. 'Well,' he sighed, glancing around the room once more, 'I believe we have squeezed this particular lemon dry, Watson. I think it's time to return to Baker Street and draw up our battle plans.'

We left the house and walked down the path. 'We will have to make our way to the main road in order to summon a cab,' observed Holmes, and then as if on cue a hansom appeared at the end of the road. I stepped out onto the pavement ready to wave it down, but Holmes pulled me back.

'I don't like the look of this one,' he muttered, staring at the cab, which I now saw was racing at quite a speed down the empty street.

I gazed at the driver's face, which was muffled by a scarf, but his eyes, wild and protuberant, were fixed on us. Then I saw a movement at the window of the cab. Before I had time to react, Holmes had dragged me backwards into the garden and pulled me to the ground behind the straggly privet hedge. As he did so, a gunshot rang out, the bullet whizzing over our heads. We heard the cab rattle past and by the time we had regained our footing, it had disappeared around the corner at the end of the road.

'Friends of Gaunt,' I observed, brushing myself down.

'Undoubtedly. You've got to give it to them, they are a very efficient organisation.'

'Not too efficient,' I smiled bleakly, 'or neither you nor I would be alive.'

'Let's hope it stays that way, Watson.'

When we returned to Baker Street there was a telegram waiting for Holmes from his brother Mycroft. Holmes read it quickly and tossed it over to me.

COME TO THE DIOGENES CLUB AT ONCE.
DEVELOPMENTS. M.

'What developments?'

'There are several possibilities, but rather than pontificate on them now, I suggest we heed Mycroft's summons. He will tell us what we need to know.'

Holmes once described the Diogenes Club to me as 'the queerest club in London'. It is the refuge of those men who for various reasons have no wish for the company of their fellows, yet these individuals are not averse to comfortable chairs and the latest periodicals in pleasant surroundings. It is for the convenience of these that the Diogenes Club was founded on Pall Mall, just down from the Carlton, and it now contains the most unsociable and unclubbable men in London. No member is permitted to take the least notice of any other. No talking is allowed under any circumstances on the premises save in the Stranger's Room.

As we mounted the steps to the front door, Holmes pressed his forefinger to his lips, indicating that I should remain silent. He then led the way into the hall. Through the glass panelling I caught a glimpse of a large and luxurious room, in which a considerable number of men were sitting about and reading papers or dozing, each in his own little nook. Holmes showed me into a small chamber, which looked out into Pall Mall, and handed a note to a passing servant.

Five minutes later Mycroft Holmes appeared. We had met several times before, but I always found it remarkable that he was so different from his brother in appearance. He was a much larger and stouter man than Sherlock. His body was corpulent, but his face, though massive, had preserved something of the sharpness of expression that was so remarkable in that of his brother. His eyes, which were of a peculiarly light, watery grey, seemed to always retain a faraway, introspective look.

'I have been waiting hours for you, Sherlock, where have you been?' he said without any preamble and with some irritation.

'Out investigating and getting shot at,' responded Holmes blithely.

Mycroft took a step back and surveyed his brother. 'Well, they obviously missed.'

'This time, yes. Your telegram mentioned developments. They have made their request?'

'Indeed they have.' Mycroft shook his head sadly. He reached into his pocket and retrieved a sheet of blue paper, which he passed to Holmes. With cool, calm consideration, his face an emotionless mask, my friend read the missive and then handed the paper to me, on which was a typewritten message:

To the British Government

To preserve you and the Royal Family from the ramifications of a national scandal and a crisis that would no doubt bring ruin to both institutions, we are prepared to suppress the information that the son of a whore has claims upon the throne for certain considerations. Think what anarchy would erupt if such information were spoken abroad. The Fenians, the anarchists and republicans who have been waiting hungrily in the wings for years would fall on this with relish. Civil conflict would most certainly result.

All this can be avoided for a one-off payment of one million pounds. A small amount to ensure peace and the status quo. No doubt you will require time to discuss this and arrange payment. We shall be in touch again in forty-eight hours.

Prince William sends his regards.

'Elegantly written,' observed Holmes almost absent-mindedly, his eyes hooded in thought.

'The missive was accompanied by a photograph of the boy.'

'A recent one?'

'Taken yesterday,' affirmed Mycroft.

'How can you be certain?'

'The child was holding a copy of yesterday's *Times*.'

Holmes pursed his lips. 'Clever. Well, at least now we know what they are after.'

'One million pounds,' I cried. 'That's outrageous!'

'Indeed. But they can afford to be audacious when they seem to hold all the cards.'

'What is more pertinent is whether you can pay the price of their silence,' said Holmes.

'Of course the British government can. But the problem with all blackmail threats is that one never knows when they will end. A million pounds this week... and next week? You have to do something, Sherlock.'

'How did this message arrive?'

'By post. It was addressed to the Prime Minister, personal and urgent. They are a very confident bunch, I will give them that, but there must be a chink in their armour.'

'If only we could find it,' observed Holmes dourly.

Twenty-Two

The tall man could not help but smile when Gaunt had relayed his various adventures concerning himself and Sherlock Holmes.

'That fellow is as slippery as a varnished eel. He seems able to ease his way out of every tight spot.' The tall man laughed. 'Although I damn him to hell, I must admit I admire his tenacity and panache.'

Gaunt was not amused. 'It might seem comic to an outsider,' he said, 'but he still remains a threat.'

The man placed an avuncular arm on Gaunt's shoulders. 'Not a really serious one, Dom. It seems that Mr Holmes's brilliance has gone off the boil somewhat. Despite all his efforts he is no nearer to finding us than he was at the beginning. He may have a facility for escaping, but he is still as much in the dark as he ever was and, I believe, ever will be.'

'I wish I had your confidence.'

'I am sensible enough to know that nothing is infallible, but our organisation is strong and powerful, with a veritable wizard at the helm. As you know, this project has been many months in the planning and arranging. We are certainly not going to be beaten by one man, even if that man is Sherlock Holmes. He has proved to be a nuisance, but we must consider him no longer so – unless, that is, he comes too close. Our focus must now return to our own machinations, not his. I am echoing the words of our master. You understand?'

Gaunt nodded gravely. 'I understand.'

'And so we have put the final stage of our plan into operation. M arranged it yesterday evening.'

'Really?' Gaunt said with a mixture of surprise and dismay. He had expected to be party to any sudden changes of strategy. After all he was one of the main players in the organisation. He believed that he would be consulted about such important decisions. But it seemed not.

The tall man sensed Gaunt's feelings. 'We really could not wait any longer. We had delayed things long enough because of Holmes. Especially now we have lost you as our mole at the Yard we need to press on. The authorities are redoubling their efforts to track us down. Army espionage agents have already been engaged to seek us out.'

'What is the current situation?'

'The Prime Minister received a communication this morning with our demand. We have given them forty-eight hours to consider it and raise the funds. In the meantime, I intend to return to London to our headquarters.'

'Why?'

'I have been called back and anyway I need to be on hand as things progress. It is imperative that I am at the centre of things.'

'What about the boy?'

'I shall take him with me. M wants him close at hand for the final sequence of the game.'

'What about me? I can't go home.'

The tall man stroked his chin thoughtfully. 'Yes. Well, we cannot risk you accompanying me – now that you are a fugitive from justice you cannot remain in this house as I'm closing it down while I'm in London. I've released most of the servants already. You'll certainly need to lie low. Every bobby on the beat will have an eye out for you now. I suggest you camp out at the Grimes's place as a temporary measure. They have the room.'

Gaunt curled his lip. 'Those dregs of humanity!'

The tall man smiled indulgently. 'It's only for a few days. Beggars can't be choosers – and after those few days you will no longer be a beggar. With a smart new set of clothes and a small fortune you will be all set to cross the Channel and start a new life as a wealthy monsieur.'

Gaunt liked the image that this description brought to his mind and he found that he was smiling too.

'We'll keep in touch in the usual fashion. No doubt when the forty-eight hours are up, things will move quickly. The fuse has been lit.'

'Where is M now?'

'Watching us all, no doubt. I spoke to him by telephone from my office yesterday. Now if you will excuse me, I must make arrangements for the journey. Stay awhile if you wish. Help yourself to brandy and then off you go to reacquaint yourself with the Grimeses.'

* * *

In London, down in his underground lair, the mastermind behind the plot was smoking a cigar and smiling. It all seemed to be going smoothly, despite the interference of Mr Sherlock Holmes, who it seemed on his present performance was losing his grip. At this thought, M emitted a dry chuckle. It was so good to combine two operations in one: draining the government's coffers of one million pounds and showing up Sherlock Holmes as a failed master detective. If he could have raised himself out of the wheelchair, M would have done a jig of triumph. The smile faded as he was reminded that his dancing days – indeed his walking days – were over. And he knew who he had to thank for that.

Twenty-Three

Dr Watson's Journal

Sherlock Holmes was silent in the cab on our way back to Baker Street after the meeting with Mycroft. Our parting had been a glum one. This was understandable for as far as I could see there were few glimmers of sunlight piercing through the dark clouds that loured over our heads. I gazed at my friend's face partly masked by the shadows, but I could see that he was deep in thought: his brows were contracted and the eyes hooded, the lips tightly drawn. However, it was more than serious contemplation that gave my friend this dark and sombre expression. I could also tell that he was very worried.

Evening was drawing in as we climbed up the stairs to our chambers. I lit the gas as Holmes retreated to his bedroom, emerging some minutes later with three large volumes, which he placed on the table in the centre of the sitting room. Straining my eyes I noted that they were some kind of gazetteer.

He lit his pipe and without a word to me began poring over them, rippling the pages with a speedy regularity. What he was seeking, I could not tell, but I had no doubt he would confide in me in due course when his search was over.

I ordered tea and sandwiches from Mrs Hudson, but Holmes refused any refreshment and merely refilled his pipe, polluting our room with a thick vapour. After devouring the ham sandwiches and tea, I began to feel drowsy. The warmth of the fire and rigours of the last twenty-four hours lulled me towards sleep. I was just on the verge of nodding off when a sharp cry of exultation from Holmes brought me back from the edge of slumber with a start.

Holmes slapped his palm down hard on the page he had been studying. 'I've got it, my boy. I've got it.'

'What on earth is it?' I said, rousing myself and moving over to the table.

'Look, look,' he said with some excitement, his elegant bony finger pointing to an illustration on the page. It was a line drawing of a fine manor house in extensive grounds. I felt a tingle of excitement as I gazed at it.

'Why, that's the house in the picture we saw in Gaunt's office and at his home.'

'Indeed it is,' replied my friend, and in the manner of a stage magician, he produced the drawing from his inside pocket and laid it flat on the table next to the book. There was no doubt about it: they were both the same property.

'Where is it?'

'It is Galworth Hall, near Richmond. A fine dwelling, built in the time of George IV for the Duke of Dartington. This volume informs me that after the duke's death in 1805, it remained untenanted for some twenty years and then was bought for a pittance by the Coates family who have owned it ever since. Currently it is the home of Sir Jasper Coates.'

'I know that name.'

'Indeed you do. He is one of the undersecretaries to the Home Secretary.'

'A member of the government!'

'Intriguing, eh? Also remember those letters we discovered in Gaunt's desk at Scotland Yard.'

'What about them?'

'They were signed...'

'Of course, with the letter "J". Jasper.'

'Precisely.'

'So what is Gaunt's connection with Sir Jasper Coates?'

'A very pertinent question, Watson. And I fully intend to discover the answer. Grab your revolver and your overcoat; we have a lengthy journey in prospect.'

'You intend to go to Galworth Hall tonight?'

'Yes. I will arrange to hire John's dog cart again.'

I nodded, remembering the business with Neville St Clair some years previously. 'But can't it wait till morning?'

'No, Watson. Time is of the essence.'

'There is obviously some connection between Sir Jasper Coates of Galworth Hall and Inspector Gaunt. Have you any notion what it might be?'

It was some thirty minutes later and we were rattling along on our way towards Richmond, which is southwest of the city in the county of Surrey. Holmes had estimated that our drive was about twelve miles. I had kept my own counsel for some time as we had dashed through the streets, which gradually widened until we were flying across a broad balustrade bridge, with the murky Thames flowing sluggishly beneath. We had driven several miles, and were beginning to reach the fringe of the belt of suburban villas, when I sensed that my companion had relaxed somewhat now that we had left the metropolis behind. This allowed me to ask the question that had been on the tip of my tongue since he had proposed this nocturnal adventure.

'There are several possibilities, but I am not in possession of sufficient data to be certain which is the most likely. However, it is remarkably suggestive that the owner of Galworth Hall is a member of Her Majesty's government. It is clear that it would be most beneficial to the organisation that we are dealing with if they had an agent close to the heart of the matter. They had one in Scotland Yard, after all.'

'You are saying that Sir Jasper Coates is a traitor.'

'Not quite, but I am saying that it is possible.'

'What do you intend to do?'

'The time for subtle actions is over, I'm afraid. I am left with little alternative but to beard the fellow in his den. It should be clear very quickly whether he is an innocent in this matter or…' He paused and flashed me a troubled glance. 'Or not,' he concluded.

We continued in silence as we drove along country roads, through scattered villages until we reached the outskirts of the small town of Richmond. Holmes reined in the horse and, lighting a dark lantern, withdrew a map from his coat pocket. He unfolded it, and we leaned over it together, his gloved finger tracing the route to our destination.

'We pass through the town and then three miles further on the road forks, you see? We take the left fork – it looks no more than a cart track up to the gates of Galworth Hall.'

Dousing the lantern we continued our journey. Holmes directed the cart as the map had indicated and in fifteen minutes we approached the great gateposts of the Hall. It was a bright, cloudless, moonlit night and we could see past the gateposts down a gently curving drive to the spectral silhouette of the house itself. Shimmering in the ghostly moonlight, it did indeed look insubstantial and dreamlike. As far as I could see there were no lights on in any of the windows.

'It looks like they are all abed,' I muttered.

'If that is the case, we shall have to wake them,' said Holmes, urging the horse forward.

We pulled up outside the house and Holmes leapt to the ground and approached the front door, leaving me to tether the horse. As I did so, he swung the large knocker vigorously on the great oak door, the sound echoing around us on the still night air.

I consulted my pocket watch. It was only a little after ten, rather early for the whole household to be asleep, but there did not seem to be any signs of life from within. Holmes continued swinging the knocker against the door. After what seemed an age, we heard a movement on the other side and then the grating of the lock. The door opened slowly to reveal a man in butler's livery, carrying an oil lamp. His back was bent with age and service and his sallow ancient features were scored with many wrinkles. His expression was a mixture of apprehension and surprise. He seemed unsure how to address us. Holmes saved him the bother.

'I am Sherlock Holmes and I am here to see your master,' he snapped, stepping forward forcefully, causing the lackey to retreat into the hallway.

'I am afraid Sir Jasper is away at the moment. He is in London for a lengthy period. All the other servants have been dismissed. There is no one else in residence. I am the sole occupant at present.'

'Has he taken the child with him?'

The butler frowned. In the dim light it was difficult to determine his real emotions. Was he shocked that Holmes knew of a child or was the man merely puzzled by Holmes's query?

'What child?' he replied after a pause.

'The little boy that Sir Jasper has been keeping here.'

The butler shook his head. 'I know of no child, sir.'

'I see,' said Holmes, revealing his pistol from the folds of his coat. 'Then we shall have to see for ourselves. Come, Watson.'

Snatching up a lighted candelabra from the hall table, Holmes strode past the bewildered butler and headed for the staircase. I followed suit. 'If the boy was kept prisoner here, it would no doubt be in one of the bedrooms,' said Holmes in hushed tones. 'Even if he has been taken there will be signs that he has been here. That will secure the link between Sir Jasper and the kidnappers.'

As swiftly and efficiently as we could, in turn we entered all the bedrooms on the first floor. Most seemed as though they had not been occupied for some time, except one that was obviously Sir Jasper's but offered up no apparent clues. We moved upstairs to the top floor of the house. There were several servants' rooms – all empty – and a large attic bedroom. An inspection of this chamber certainly bore fruit.

'The boy has been here,' cried Holmes, holding up a sheaf of childish drawings that had been strewn on the bed. He moved to the bedside cabinet and took up an empty glass that was resting there and raised it to his nose and sniffed. 'Morphine. The boy was sedated, probably in preparation for his journey.'

'Where have they taken him?'

Holmes shrugged. 'Probably not Sir Jasper's townhouse. That would be too dangerous.'

'Do you think the servant will know?'

'No. It is clear to me that he has no knowledge of this affair. From his response to my queries, it seems unlikely that he was even aware that there was a young boy on the premises. It would be easy to keep him in the dark.'

'So we are no further in our investigations.'

'Oh, yes, I think we can be a little more sanguine, old fellow. Sir Jasper is obviously a key player in the conspiracy and it should not be too difficult to track him down. But first I think a thorough search of Sir Jasper's private quarters before we return to London.'

In his meticulous and remarkably thorough fashion, Sherlock Holmes examined Sir Jasper's chamber, a large well-furnished apartment used, it seemed to me, as a business office. The butler, still bewildered by our presence, confirmed that this was the room Sir Jasper used when working on government matters. With magnifying glass in hand, Holmes ranged around the room in search of clues, even crawling about on the carpet when he seemed to have noticed something of interest. He was completely absorbed and did not utter a word to me as he carried out his investigations. The main focus of his search was the rather elegant escritoire situated by the window. The drawers were locked and Holmes had to force them open. However, while they contained many private papers, they mostly dealt with estate business, minor government matters and there were a few tailor's bills and a wine merchant's account. 'Nothing here concerning the boy or his cohorts in the kidnapping,' growled Holmes, disappointment etched on his face.

'Maybe he kept all that material in his townhouse.'

'I suspect you are right. That must be our next port of call but, before we depart, I'd like a further word with our butler friend.'

The servant was greatly perturbed by our visit and somewhat

disorientated. Holmes leaned close to me and whispered, 'Poor devil. He's more in the dark about things than we are.'

The old fellow virtually stood to attention as we approached, his ancient features contorted with apprehension.

'What is your name?' asked Holmes, not unkindly.

'Barrow, sir.'

'I have just a few questions to ask you, Barrow, and then we shall be on our way.'

Barrow blinked like a frightened owl.

'Your master has many visitors?'

'No, not many, sir. He entertains little here. Most of his social engagements are in London.'

'However, he has received a visitor recently, who came in a wheelchair.'

Barrow's face softened and his eyes flashed in recognition. 'Oh, yes, sir, Mr Moore I believe is the gentleman's name.'

'Moore? Can you describe him?'

'Not very precisely, I am afraid. He is an invalid, you understand. The gentleman wore dark glasses and kept his hat on indoors and of course, being wheelchair-bound, he was wrapped up quite well.'

'What age would you say he was?'

Barrow pursed his lips while he considered his answer. 'It is difficult to be accurate, I'm afraid. He was not young. His voice was quite frail, rather strange and croaky. Maybe he was somewhere in his late fifties. Possibly sixties. I really couldn't be more precise.'

'Is there anything else unusual about this man you can tell me? This is very important.'

The butler's face clouded for a moment. I could see that he was desperate to provide Holmes with some titbit of information that would remove him from this tortuous rack of interrogation.

'There is nothing really, sir...' he said at length and then paused.

'But yet...' prompted Holmes, thrusting his face closer to him.

'Well... his wheelchair was rather... unusual.'

'Unusual? In what way?'

'It was self-propelled. It had some kind of motor device fitted that allowed Mr Moore to move without any effort. He didn't have to physically roll the wheels as is usually the case with those contraptions.'

'Mmm,' said Holmes, visibly disappointed in this information. 'And there is nothing else about the man that you can remember?'

'No, sir. I saw little of him. Just to accompany him to Sir Jasper's office... that's all.'

'Office? So he was here on business. It was not a social call?'

'I assume so. I am afraid Sir Jasper does not confide in me on such matters.'

'Very well,' said Holmes, drawing back from the old retainer and turning to me. 'I think our usefulness here is at an end, Watson. Time for us to return to the metropolis.' So saying, he took hold of my arm and marched towards the door.

Twenty-Four

'The boy is safely stowed?' Sir Jasper Coates asked.

The professor manoeuvred his wheelchair out of the shadows into the light.

'He is sleeping in the room I have prepared for him.'

'That is good.'

'Indeed.' The professor smiled benignly. His lips curved gently, but the eyes remained icy and still. 'You have completed your role in this affair with great effect, Sir Jasper. You are to be congratulated on your dedication and attention to detail.' His voice escaped as a harsh whisper.

Sir Jasper gave an imperceptible nod of the head.

'However,' continued the professor, still smiling, 'it has to be noted that as from this moment your duties and indeed your usefulness are at an end.'

A look of mild confusion came over the knight's face. Was this some kind of subtle jest? Surely it was. He smiled in anticipation of a light-hearted joke.

It was not forthcoming.

Instead, the professor withdrew a revolver from under the rug covering his legs. 'It has long been a maxim of mine, that when something – or someone – has ceased to be essential to one's plans, it is best that they are eliminated. It clears the decks – as sailors say.'

Sir Jasper stiffened and his mouth opened as though he was about to speak, but so stunned was he by this sudden and dramatic turn of events that he could not bring forth any words.

'Again, I thank you for your efforts and cooperation. I could not have asked for more. And indeed you are not able to offer more – and so now it is goodbye.' He aimed the pistol at Sir Jasper and fired. Before the knight had time to move, time to plead, time to turn and run, the bullet ripped through his heart. His body shuddered with the impact and then he uttered one brief gargling croak, his hand clasping his chest as thin rivulets of blood trickled over the fingers. Coates gazed at his assailant, his eyes wide with shock, and then silently he fell forward on to his face.

Moriarty slipped the gun back under the rug. This time his smile was genuine and the amusement reached his eyes.

The door of the chamber opened and Dominic Gaunt entered. He gazed down at the corpse, his face a mask of indifference.

'Just tidying up some unfinished business,' said the professor.

'So I see and indeed, heard.'

'I'm relying on you to dispose of the body in the usual way.'

'It was necessary then?'

'Indeed. Coates was too significant a character in our machinations for me to allow him to live. His position in society and within the government would always make him vulnerable and thus a threat to us. It was essential to eliminate him once his usefulness was over. Ah, but you look sad. You were fond of him?'

'After a fashion. He had charm and was amusing. A passing fancy.'

Moriarty nodded as though in agreement. 'It is as well. Personal attachments are not for the likes of us. They complicate matters. Besides, Sir Jasper Coates was not of our breed, my dear Gaunt. He was a zealot. A man with a cause and a possessor of high if rather misguided principles. He really believed we would bring about the downfall of the government. Misguided and naive. Not like you and I: mere criminals. Seekers of wealth. The collectors of ill-gotten gains.' The professor laughed heartily, his thin body rippling in his chair while the sound emerged like the expulsion of a damaged bellows.

'Mere criminals?' repeated Gaunt jauntily. 'I think not. Certainly not in your case. Are you not the Napoleon of Crime?'

'Well, I was once, before I acquired this crippled body. That will teach me to go swimming in Switzerland.' He laughed again, but this time there was sharp bitterness to the merriment. 'However, once this particular venture is brought to a happy conclusion with the noses of both Scotland Yard and Sherlock Holmes well and truly rubbed in the dirt, I will feel like wearing my old appellation again.'

'That will be soon.'

'Sooner than you think.'

'What do you mean?'

'Never allow the enemy to know exactly what you are doing. They think we have given them forty-eight hours. They have been misled. We will inform them at noon that we need a decision by midnight. I will ring through to the Prime Minister now that we have his special number, thanks to the previously invaluable Sir

Jasper. That should put the cat well and truly in their pigeon coop.'

'Indeed, it should.'

'Now, Gaunt, do get rid of this body. The sight of it is beginning to offend me.'

Twenty-Five

Dr Watson's Journal

The fire had taken hold of the building by the time Holmes and I arrived. The firemen were fighting a losing battle against the voracious flames as they consumed the structure, making it their own. Dawn was breaking and it seemed that the glow of the conflagration was merging with the rosy tint of the morning sky, creating one uniform fiery firmament. There was a large crowd of goggle-eyed onlookers building up around the cordon created by the fire fighters to keep them away from the flames. Despite shouted injunctions to 'stay back for safety's sake', the spectators edged forward, mesmerised by the rippling inferno.

Holmes and I stood in the background watching as the roof of the two-storey townhouse eventually surrendered to the flames and came crashing down inside the shell of the building, sending a fusillade of sparks heavenwards.

'My goodness, this is terrible, Holmes,' I cried. 'Do you think Sir Jasper is in there – and the boy?'

'I would think not. It is most likely that this fire was started deliberately.'

'For what reason?'

'Sir Jasper's role in the kidnap plot would soon become known. He has no future as a public figure. Perhaps he was intent on eradicating his past... or...'

Holmes paused, his features revealing that a sudden strange thought had struck him.

'Or... what?' I prompted.

'Or... his master was. There may be secrets in that house that needed to be destroyed. We found none at Galworth Hall.'

I gazed for a moment at the burning house, now a mere crumbling skeleton of a structure at the heart of the inferno. 'So, we are yet again a few steps behind them,' I said.

Holmes touched my shoulder, his own body slumping with fatigue. 'Once again you are correct. Brutally so. All along in this case I seem to be following in the wake of the villains – never quite getting them within my sights. Hah, it may be that this time I have met my match. Another Moriarty.'

'I know how you revered Moriarty as a criminal genius, but you beat him in the end and you will prevail against whoever is behind this villainy. With your brains and just a piece of good luck...'

Holmes gave a bitter chuckle. 'Well, the luck does not seem to be coming my way and perhaps the brain is atrophying...'

'That could indeed be the case,' observed a voice from someone standing behind us.

We both turned to see the not inconsiderable bulk of Mycroft Holmes. His face, tinged pink by the reflection of the fire, was twisted into an expression of great displeasure.

'What on earth are you doing here?' I found myself saying

before I had really considered the question.

'Sir Jasper is a member of the government and as such one of Mycroft's flock,' said Holmes. 'In the current dramatic circumstances as soon as the authorities learned of this fire, Mycroft would have been contacted.'

'That is so. I do not take kindly to being woken in the middle of the night and then being forced to emerge in the darkling hours to attend a bonfire. What do you know, Sherlock?'

'Sir Jasper is one of the kidnap gang.'

'A traitor.'

Holmes nodded. 'A mole. Either he has gone to ground and destroyed any clues his house could offer or...'

'Or his masters have eliminated him. Maybe presented him as a burnt offering.' Mycroft nodded towards the fire.

'You never suspected Sir Jasper?' I asked.

'Only of being too charming. I suppose that should have alerted me. While his whereabouts are of some concern, more importantly, where is the boy? Time, my dear Sherlock, is running out.'

Holmes tapped his cane impatiently on the pavement. 'Statements of the obvious are of little use to me, Mycroft. Please desist from uttering them.'

'Then please demonstrate that you are actually doing something to bring this business to a satisfactory conclusion.'

'Holmes is doing his best,' I snapped, unable to resist defending my friend.

Mycroft gave me one of his supercilious smiles. 'Then perhaps his best is not quite good enough.'

Holmes sighed. 'We are wasting time in this badinage. I have matters that await my attention elsewhere.' My friend turned and beckoned me to join him as he strode off at a brisk pace.

'I appreciate your comments in my defence,' Holmes said, when I had caught up with him, 'but I am well able to fight my own battles, especially against my brother. Remember, I know him of old from the nursery to manhood. Whenever things are not quite going his way, he lashes out at others, blaming their incompetence, especially with me. Many are the times in our youth when he railed against me in order that I would assist him to achieve his own ends. The same applies today. His recent outburst was based on fear and frustration rather than any criticism of me. This kidnap business is really eating away at *his* confidence.'

'And not yours?' I said softly.

Holmes gave me a soft smile. 'Touché, Watson. A palpable hit. Certainly, I must confess that I am not at ease, but I have not as yet given up hope.'

'Where to now, then?'

'Back to Baker Street. A wash, a shave and a hearty breakfast to revive the tired spirit. I have an exhausting morning ahead of me I think – but I will not require your services, so I suggest that you rest yourself in readiness for more rigours ahead.'

'Are you sure that I cannot be of assistance?' I asked, unable to keep the dismay from my voice. I was unhappy at the prospect of being left out of the next development in this dark and difficult case, keen to be present at all the stages of the investigation.

'In this instance, yes. Fear not, if I am successful all will be revealed. Take heart, old fellow; you know I treasure your company and assistance, but there are times when it is best that I act alone.'

I nodded. I could not deny the veracity of his words, but this fact did not cheer me.

* * *

Two hours later we had breakfasted and refreshed our toilet. While I had devoured bacon, scrambled eggs and toast, Holmes had merely toyed with some toast and smoked several of yesterday's dottles, filling our sitting room with a thin, pungent veil. As I settled down by the fire with a cup of coffee and attempted to peruse a medical journal in the vain hope I could distract my thoughts, he donned his overcoat once more and bid me au revoir.

'With luck, I hope to return by lunchtime.'

'I wish you well.'

He gave me a brief salute and departed.

I sat for some time, staring blindly into the distance, while my coffee grew cold and the forgotten journal slid from my lap onto the hearthrug. My mind was awhirl with ideas, worries and myriad ruminations all concerned with our investigations, the tangled skein that had enmeshed us and indeed those higher than ourselves. It seemed to me that, for all our efforts, we were really no closer to finding the kidnapped boy or apprehending the villains behind the nefarious scheme.

I ran through the series of events in chronological order, reminding myself of each twist and turn, in a desperate attempt to see if I could unearth one clue that I might have missed along the way. But my efforts were fruitless. There was no sudden shaft of light illuminating my darkness. Neither could I fathom what errand Holmes was about this morning, one in which, as he put it, he would not 'require my services'. Despite Holmes's explanations, I still felt hurt at being removed from the chase at this crucial stage.

Suddenly, I felt very tired. A full stomach and a warm fire, along with a weary brain, gradually lulled me towards sleep. However, I was awoken by raised voices and the sound of hurried footsteps on the stairs. Moments later the door burst open and Ronald Temple propelled himself into the room. He was unshaven and his whole appearance was one of neglect. His tie was askew, his clothes rumpled and his eyes bleary from lack of sleep.

Behind him I could see the figure of Mrs Hudson, her face flushed and her hands fluttering wildly. 'I told the gentleman that Mr Holmes was not at home, but he wouldn't listen to me,' she said apologetically.

'That's quite all right, Mrs Hudson. I'll attend to our visitor,' I said, rising from my chair.

She nodded, gave a pinched look at the recalcitrant intruder and closed the door.

'Where the devil is he?' snapped Temple, once we were alone. 'Why have we heard nothing? Don't you know the hell we're going through?'

'You are all but done in, Mr Temple. Take a seat, please and I'll get you a brandy.'

'I don't want brandy. I want answers,' he snapped, but his fatigue overcame him at that moment and he collapsed into the wicker chair. I poured him a small brandy and despite his earlier protestations, he drank it in one gulp.

'What on earth is going on?' he asked at last, all the fire of his temper having dissipated. Here was a tired and desperate man, eager to hear news, good news, about his son. Suddenly I felt guilty. In concentrating on the case at hand, both Holmes and I had neglected our client. It was true that there was very little we could tell him – certainly we had nothing positive to impart – but I realised that we should have made some effort to contact the family to reassure them that we were expending all our energies in pursuit of a successful conclusion to the case. To have heard nothing must have been wretched for them. As I gazed at this distraught and desperate creature I felt ashamed.

In a humble and less than fully coherent fashion, I apologised for our silence, assuring him that this was because we had been concentrating all our efforts in following various leads.

'And have you made some headway? Are you nearer to finding our son?' he asked, his voice breaking and his tired bloodshot eyes moistening with emotion.

'We are hopeful,' I said. 'Mr Holmes is out on the trail of some information now. If anyone can find your boy it is he.'

'And what if no one can?' he retorted bitterly.

'Do not give up hope, Mr Temple. It is very rare that Sherlock Holmes fails.'

'Rare, but not unknown, eh?'

I sighed. I realised there was little chance that I could reassure our distressed client.

'If only you could see my wife, Dr Watson. She does not eat or sleep. Her face is haggard with anguish and she spends most of her time weeping. Neither I nor her sister can comfort her.'

My heart went out to this poor fellow. I would have done anything in the world to help him, to be able to confirm without doubt that we should return his son within the day. But I could not.

I rose and patted him on the shoulder. 'It remains a waiting game, I am afraid, but we are expecting developments shortly. I promise you that we shall be in touch with you within the next twenty-four hours to keep you abreast of matters. I pray that then we shall be able to bring you good news.'

Temple looked blankly at me as though all the spirit had been sucked out of him. With hunched shoulders he got to his feet and in a shambling fashion he made his way to the door. Without another word or a glance back at me, he departed. I felt wretched that I had not been able to give him more than vague promises. I realised, not for the first time, that when Holmes and I were engrossed in an investigation, we often forgot that the events that were fascinating and stimulating us could be having heartbreaking effects on those at the centre of the affair.

In very low spirits, I poured myself a brandy and resumed my seat by the fire to wait for Holmes's return, desperately hoping that he would bring positive tidings with him.

Twenty-Six

Although Sherlock Holmes valued and respected Watson's assistance while investigating a case, there were times when he preferred to operate alone. Watson had a grand gift of silence and was invaluable in a crisis, but there were occasions when Holmes felt the need to act on his own. He could work more swiftly, not having to take a confederate into consideration and, more practically, he could fail without an audience. His mission that morning was built on the most tenuous of threads and he had only the slightest of hopes that it would bear fruit. As a consequence, he wanted to explore this slender avenue quickly and without the encumbrance of a companion.

His mission was to visit the various manufacturers of wheelchairs in the City of London in search of the establishment that constructed the mechanical model described by Sir Jasper Coates's butler. Holmes was convinced that the owner of that wheelchair was the key figure in the affair. He had constructed a list of such companies from *Addison's Business Companion* and so he began the tedious round of suppliers. At first he met with ignorance or disinterest at all the places he visited. However, around mid-morning, he called at Mortimer's Invalid Conveyances in Chelsea. It was a small firm, which had a shop area attached to the workshop.

Holmes entered the shop and was greeted by a fresh-faced, enthusiastic young man, dressed almost in the manner of an undertaker, but his bright eyes and energetic attitude suggested a far sunnier outlook. Holmes deduced that this was the fellow's first job and he had not been in it for very long. His trousers still had the sharp crease of newness and the elbows of his jacket showed none of the shine that comes with regular wear.

However, when Holmes explained what he was looking for, the brightness dimmed in the young man's demeanour.

'We have nothing like that, sir,' he said, shaking his head. 'Mortimer's is a traditional firm. We have been making invalid conveyances for over a hundred years and have in that time supplied such items to members of the gentry and the aristocracy. We have a standard range, but we also offer the facility for bespoke models should you so desire.' It was a speech the young man had learned off pat. Holmes wondered how many times a day he repeated it.

'Bespoke – but not motorised.'

The young man shook his head. 'I am afraid old Mr Mortimer does not hold with such contraptions. They are very rare and he believes they will be a passing fad.' Suddenly the young man leaned forward in a conspiratorial fashion and lowered his voice. 'In my opinion, sir, Mr Mortimer is wrong. I believe that is where the future lies for invalid conveyances. A motorised chair gives the occupant much more independence. They will become very popular in time, I am convinced of it.'

Holmes nodded enthusiastically. 'If I wanted to get hold of one of these contraptions today, where would I go?'

The young man pursed his lips. Holmes could see that he was fully aware that there was no sale in prospect for him, but would he be prepared to pass on information that would lead him to another supplier?

'Well, sir,' he said at length, still maintaining his conspiratorial tone, 'at present there are no major manufacturers producing such chairs, but I do know of an inventor-type fellow who has made a few for certain clients. He is an eccentric old chap but brilliant. I'd love him to come and work here, but he'd never do that. And Mr Mortimer wouldn't agree to it anyway.'

'But he may be prepared to make me one of these motorised chairs.'

'For a certain fee, I have no doubt about it.'

'Who is this fellow?'

The young man glanced nervously around him before snatching up a piece of paper from below the counter and scribbling something on it.

'I would be obliged, sir, that you do not mention how you obtained this name and address. If Mr Mortimer found out I would most likely lose my job.'

Holmes smiled kindly. 'Your secret is safe with me,' he said, holding out his hand. The young man passed him the paper. It bore the words 'Ralph Harbottle, 5 Angel Court'.

'Thank you,' said Holmes, touching the brim of his hat.

Within five minutes he was in a hansom cab on route to Angel Court.

* * *

It was just after noon when Sherlock Holmes found himself in a cab returning to Baker Street. His face was drawn and pale and, despite all his efforts, he could not stop his hands from shaking. He could not deny that his morning's activities had certainly borne fruit, but they had also unearthed information that had shocked him to the core. Holmes was rarely surprised by events to such a violent extent and the experience was unpleasant. It was difficult to believe and yet he knew in his heart of hearts that what he had learned, what he had deduced, must be the truth – the terrible truth.

'We're here, guv'nor.' The cabby's cry broke through the thick cloud of swirling thoughts in the detective's mind.

Holmes left the cab in a kind of trance and after paying his fare, he stood before the door of 221B Baker Street for some moments before entering. As he made his way up to the sitting room, one thing that helped to buoy him up was the thought that he would be able to share his news with Watson.

Twenty-Seven

Dr Watson's Journal

The Sherlock Holmes who walked through our sitting-room door shortly after noon that day was far from the keen-faced sleuth-hound I had been expecting. Even after a night without sleep, he had left that morning eager and alert, his features taut with expectation. The man who appeared before me now was pale of feature and seemed weary, as though the worries of the world had been heaped upon his shoulders. It was clear to me that something terrible had happened in the interim and my heart was filled with dark forebodings. Casting off his coat, my friend slumped down in the chair opposite me without a word.

'Great heavens,' I cried, 'what on earth's the matter? You look terrible.'

Holmes gave me a wan smile. 'I've had a bit of a shock, that's all.'

'It's not the boy, is it? They've not...?' I couldn't bear to utter the words.

'No, no. Nothing like that.'

'Praise be. Well, then, what is it?'

Holmes reached for the mantelpiece and scooped up his old briar and stuffed it with tobacco before answering. 'I think I'd better tell you from the beginning.'

'Very well, please do.'

He lit his pipe and began. 'My errand this morning was to track down the supplier of the wheelchair that Sir Jasper's butler informed us about. Through them I hoped to reach the owner himself, who I believe is the brains behind this whole kidnap business. Now I know for certain that he is.'

I leaned forward in my chair in surprise and excitement. 'Really?'

'Oh, yes,' he replied darkly and puffed heavily on his pipe, sending a dark cloud of smoke forth from the bowl. 'At first I seemed to be making no progress in my enquiries whatsoever. Motorised wheelchairs are rare it seems, and regarded with either suspicion or disdain by most manufacturers. However I learned from a bright young fellow at one of the places I visited of a man called Ralph Harbottle who has invented such a model as was described to us. So I visited this Harbottle to see what I could discover about Coates's mysterious cohort.

'Harbottle's establishment is situated in a small court in Chelsea. It resembles a junk shop rather than a place of creation, but on entering the premises I observed various forms of mechanical devices, clockwork motors and such about the place. Harbottle is a plump individual who could easily have been the model for Phiz's drawings of Mr Pickwick: short with a large egg-shaped head which is bald on the top but surrounded by a mass of wild straw-coloured hair, which seems to explode horizontally from the side of his head. He was dressed in a green velvet smoking jacket and black and white dog-toothed trousers and gazed at the world through a pair of small gold-rimmed glasses. His somewhat eccentric mode of dress was reflected in his actions and speech patterns. He moved rather like a mechanical toy and he spoke quickly in short bursts with long pauses between.

'I told him the reason for my visit and he seemed delighted that I had heard of his invention, which he called "the self-propelling bath chair". I asked him how many he had made.

'"Three," came his response, "including the prototype that I have kept myself for demonstration purposes."

'"So you have had two paying customers?" I asked, and he nodded. "How did they hear of your invention?"

'He chuckled. "I have a certain reputation for those interested in unusual devices," he said. "People seek me out for all kinds of things. I have tried to interest a number of bath chair manufacturers in my design, but they all seem reticent to dip their toe into that particular pool."

'"May I ask the names of the two individuals who have purchased your mechanical bath chair?" I enquired. Harbottle grinned like a cheeky schoolboy. "You may ask, of course. We live in a liberal society." I asked whether he would furnish me with the names and he in turn asked me why I was so curious. "It is of the utmost importance that I track down the owner of one of these devices," I explained. "I have information to impart to him of the most crucial and delicate nature. I am afraid I cannot reveal more to you than that without breaking a solemn promise made to a dying man."

'Harbottle seemed to enjoy my subterfuge. His eyebrows hovered over the rim of his glasses and his eyes widened with suppressed pleasure. "How dramatic," he said. "Deliciously romantic. Well, sir, the two recipients of my machine are Lady Emilia Forsythe and a gentleman whom I only know as Mr Moore."

"'Ah," said I. 'The person I need to contact is a man and therefore it is Mr Moore that I seek." I asked him for an address, but Harbottle shook his head. "I fear not. He was a very secretive fellow and did all his business with me direct – here on my premises. He came and went like a wraith, sir. Appearing and disappearing without warning. A strange cove, indeed, but he paid well."

'I asked whether Harbottle could at least describe the man, and Harbottle frowned. "I can, after a fashion," he said. "There was very little of him that was visible to describe. He wore dark glasses and a large hat, which shaded his face. He spoke in a strange strangulated fashion. Actually, he apologised for his speech. He said that it was the result of an awful accident, the same accident that was responsible for him losing the use of his legs."

"'How old was he?" I asked, and Harbottle shrugged. "It is difficult to say. His face – the part that was visible at least – was pale and parchment-like, which would denote a man in his sixties, but his manner was, if not exactly lively, energetic and focused. There was one very strange thing about him though... All the while he was in my presence, his head kept moving from side to side rather like the waving of a poppy in the wind."

'As he said this, Watson, I felt an ice-cold shiver run the length of my spine. "Or like a reptile?" I suggested.

'Harbottle mimed the actions as I stared at him, horrified. "Indeed, sir, yes, yes. Quite apt. Very much like a reptile."'

Holmes leaned forward, his features taut with emotion. 'You see what this means, Watson.'

'My God, Moriarty,' I said.

'Moriarty,' he repeated in husky tones.

'But... that is impossible.'

My friend shook his head. 'It is not impossible. And when you have eliminated the impossible...'

'It beggars belief.'

'Well, it certainly does that. I am still having a problem fully comprehending and accepting the situation, but all the evidence points to the fact that Professor James Moriarty is alive, that he survived the waters of the Reichenbach Falls.'

'How could he survive?'

'He is a remarkable man.'

'But no man is indestructible.'

'And patently neither is he. It is obvious that while his brain may be as active as ever, physically he is very much a damaged creature, resigned to a life in a wheelchair. He must have suffered great physical hurt amongst the rocks at the base of those terrible falls.'

'And now he has come back to haunt us.'

Holmes gave a bitter chuckle. 'To taunt us, more like. And with the most cunning and outrageous plan of his whole career. Hah, I knew there was a brilliant brain behind this whole operation, one that was as devious and cunning as it is ruthless and dynamic, I just never contemplated that it could be Moriarty...'

'Why should you? The world believed that he was dead.'

'But I should have looked beyond the obvious. The signs were there. I have been as blind as a beetle. This kidnapping case bears all the hallmarks of the way he operates, even to the point of eliminating his own operatives like Sir Jasper Coates when they have ceased to be of use to him. He may be in a wheelchair, but Moriarty is still a devilish force to be reckoned with.'

For some moments we sat in silence. I, like Holmes, was completely astounded at the news that the professor was still alive and plying his damned trade once more. Holmes had called him the Napoleon of Crime, a fellow as brilliant as himself in matters of criminal activity, only the professor had chosen to travel the dark unlawful road.

'What do we do now?' I asked at length.

'We find him and this time we end his nefarious career for good. I shall not be able to sleep easily in my bed as long as that villain breathes the same air as me. Once I said that if I were certain that I could bring about the professor's demise, I would happily sacrifice my own life in the pursuit of such a goal. I am happy to repeat such a pledge.'

'It is not essential that one follows the other.'

'You are right, Watson, of course.'

'How on earth do we track him down and put an end to this threat he has over the British government and the royal family?'

'We must find his lair.'

'How?'

'That, my dear Watson, is a three-pipe problem. Please give me some time to smoke and contemplate. I have a few notions that may bear fruit if I can knock my shocked brain into action and just muse on them for an hour or so in the company of a strong shag tobacco.'

A t the same time as Sherlock Holmes was curling up in his armchair with a Persian slipper of tobacco on his lap and his head shrouded in clouds of dark grey smoke, deep in contemplation, Mycroft Holmes was seated in the Prime Minister's office along with the Home Secretary hearing of the latest developments in the Temple kidnapping case.

'It seems, gentlemen, that our enemies have changed the rules,' the Prime Minister observed gravely, leaning forward, his features weary and drained. 'Unfortunately, it is their prerogative, I am afraid. They hold the whip hand. In simple terms, they have cut short our time. I have been informed that they now require their money by midnight tonight.'

The two other men said nothing but their sombre expressions spoke volumes.

'I received a telephone call at noon giving me strict instructions concerning what has to be done,' continued the Prime Minister. 'We are to take a million pounds in notes in an unmarked carriage to a particular location on the Farnborough Road. The carriage should be driven by one man only and there must be no other accompaniment. The speaker made no secret that the money would then be transferred to several other conveyances that will disperse to various ports to leave the country. He stressed that no attempt must be made to apprehend these conveyances or news agencies around the world will be informed about the boy's parentage and claim upon the throne of England.'

'We have no guarantees they will not do that anyway,' said the Home Secretary.

The Prime Minster nodded. 'I know. That is our cleft stick, I am afraid. I cannot in all conscience ignore their demands while at the same time I am fully aware that we may very well be dupes in this matter. It may be their intention to take the money and ruin us. However, I cannot see any alternative but to take the risk. Unless you two have any brighter ideas than mine. I was told that the child would be released to us twenty-four hours after the transaction. As I stated earlier: they hold the whip hand.'

'We will have to get in touch with the Bank and arrange for the payment,' said the Home Secretary.

The Prime Minister gave a slight nod of the head and turned his gaze on Mycroft. 'I suppose you have heard nothing from your brother?'

'No, I am afraid not.'

'And there has also been profound silence from Scotland Yard and our intelligence services. We really have got our backs to the wall.'

'I will get in touch with Sherlock as soon as this meeting is over. He does tend to play his cards close to his chest, I'm afraid. It is possible that he has made some progress in his investigations…'

'And not seen fit to let us know?' snapped the Home Secretary.

'That is his way.'

The Home Secretary gave an angry snarl. 'Ridiculous,' he said.

'It would be if he was not successful in his ventures,' responded Mycroft calmly.

'He does not seem to be so very successful on this occasion.'

'Gentlemen, gentlemen,' interrupted the Prime Minister. 'Now is not the time to fall out amongst ourselves or to apportion blame. I am sure that Sherlock Holmes and the others in our service are doing their best, but we do not now have the luxury of time to wait for them to make headway. Mycroft, I need you to organise the transport side of things. The conveyance and a trusted driver must be ready by this evening. If you will see to that before you attempt to contact your brother...'

'Of course, Prime Minister.'

'Good. I must away to the palace to inform Her Majesty of the situation and you, Home Secretary...'

'I will visit the governor of the Bank and pass on the good news,' he said sourly.

Twenty-Nine

Dr Watson's Journal

Viewed from the outside, Reading Gaol was a grim-looking establishment, but it was considerably more so inside. Passing through the great oak doors, one immediately became conscious of the chill of the place and the bleak eerie silence that permeated the whole building. Despite the gaol being crammed with prisoners, none of them were allowed to talk except briefly during the exercise period once a day. They were effectively mute for most of their incarceration.

Holmes and I were shown to the governor's office by a surly uniformed guard whose attitude to us was as brusque and ill-mannered as it no doubt was to his charges. We were shown into a well-furnished panelled room with a log fire blazing in the hearth. It was the one warm spot in the whole building. The governor, Samuel McCafferty, a smart, well-made man in his late forties, rose from behind his desk to greet us.

'Well, Mr Holmes,' he said, shaking my friend's hand heartily, 'this is indeed an honour. Of course I know of your sterling work in the field of crime detection. And you must be Dr Watson, the fellow who writes up the cases.'

I nodded, indicating that I was indeed "the fellow who writes up the cases".

'Now do sit down and tell me the purpose for your visit.'

We did as we were bidden. 'It is very good of you to see us at such short notice. As I intimated in my note, our errand is one of the utmost importance,' said Holmes. 'Indeed it is a matter of national security and I am afraid I cannot divulge any of the details.'

'Good gracious,' said McCafferty with some surprise. 'You do make it sound very dramatic. But if you are not able to tell me the reason for your visit, how on earth am I able to help you?'

'I want to interview one of your inmates.'

'I see. And who might that be?'

'Colonel Sebastian Moran.'

The governor sat back in his chair with surprise. 'Really. I thought you would have done with that fellow. Didn't he try to kill you last year?'

'Indeed he did. I was instrumental in his being apprehended by the law and gave evidence at his trial.'

'So why on earth do you want to speak to him now?'

'As I intimated, the matter must remain secret. I believe that Moran has knowledge that could be of the greatest importance to me in my current investigation. I might add that this has been sanctioned by the Prime Minister. You have my word on that. So, if you could arrange for me to have access to Moran.'

The governor stared at Holmes for some moments, his face a bland mask so that it was difficult to know what he was thinking.

'Of course I believe you, Mr Holmes, and I appreciate that you would not be here if the matter was not of grave import. I will try to help you, but first of all I must warn you that you may have great difficulty in eliciting any evidence from Moran.'

'Oh, why is that?'

'Since Moran has been here, his mental condition has deteriorated rapidly. It is a common development in those who have led a privileged existence before being incarcerated. The contrast between their old life of comfort and freedom and the harsh regime of prison is too much for them to bear and their mental faculties begin to crumble. It is a kind of escape from the grim reality of their new situation. Old lags who spend their lives in and out of gaol cope much better.' He gave an ironic smile. 'This place is like a second home to them. But for Moran and his ilk, it is a kind of hell.'

'I understand,' said Holmes soberly. 'But I have to try.'

The governor leaned forward and pressed a button on his desk and within seconds the gruff orderly who had accompanied us to the room entered.

'Ah, Beaumont, will you arrange for Prisoner 142 to be taken to the safe room. These gentlemen are here to see him.'

Beaumont gave a stern nod and departed.

'It is a rule of the prison, Mr Holmes, that one of our guards must be present when prisoners receive visitors. This is for their own protection in case the prisoner in question becomes violent.'

'I understand.'

'However, with Moran I do not think you are in any danger. Any fire he had in his belly has dissipated long ago – but one cannot be too careful.'

Within five minutes, Beaumont was leading us down a series of gloomy corridors. Holmes had explained to me in Baker Street that he believed that Professor Moriarty would have returned to his secret headquarters that he had used many years ago, before the Reichenbach incident. It was from here that he had controlled his powerful organisation. 'His lair was never discovered at the time his gang was scuppered and of course the police lost interest in locating it after his death – or what they thought was his death. It would be an ideal base for his operations in this kidnapping scheme. Colonel Sebastian Moran, Moriarty's lieutenant, is the only man likely to know the location of the place. If we can squeeze that information out of him, we will be so much closer to bringing this case to a successful conclusion.'

Of course these words were uttered before we knew of Moran's mental deterioration. A mood of gloom settled down upon me once more as we entered the safe room. It was a bare windowless chamber with just one chair. This was occupied by a man in prison uniform, including a cloth cap that had a flap that fell down over the face obscuring the features. All prisoners wore these so that they could not see the faces of the other inmates. It was another measure to reduce their humanity. This procedure seemed to me an unnecessary and cruel indignity to men who, despite their crimes, were suffering greatly in the harsh conditions that were served up by the prison system.

Beaumont slammed the door shut, the sound reverberating noisily around the room, but the prisoner did not move, did not react at all. Holmes and I stood before his cowed figure.

'Can he remove his cap?' asked Holmes.

Beaumont nodded stiffly. 'Prisoner 142. Remove your cap.'

Slowly, in a jerky mechanical fashion, the man obeyed the instruction. The face that was now revealed to us hardly resembled the man I remembered from the trial. Gone was the air of bruised arrogance and smouldering spark of defiance in those piercing blue eyes. They were now hooded and milky, the pupils moving sluggishly. The whole stance of his body was one of submission and defeat.

'Colonel Moran...' said Holmes quietly and paused. There was no response, not even the flicker of an eyelid.

'He will not have been addressed in that manner since he came here. Isn't that so, Prisoner 142?' observed Beaumont.

The head now turned slowly towards the speaker.

'See,' said Beaumont, with an arrogant grin.

Holmes persisted. 'Colonel Sebastian Moran. That is you,' he said, placing a hand on the prisoner's shoulder.

The face registered no interest or recognition.

'Colonel Sebastian Moran, late of the Indian Army, and Chief of Staff to Professor Moriarty. Professor James Moriarty.'

Moran's eyes flickered at the repetition of Moriarty's name and his tongue moistened his lips.

'You remember Professor Moriarty, don't you, Moran? The professor.' Holmes leaned close, his eyes on a level with the prisoner. 'And you remember me too, Sherlock Holmes. Sherlock Holmes, the man you tried to shoot from the empty house. You remember, don't you?'

Slowly Moran's face showed some movement: the muscles round the eyes twitched slightly and his lips quivered. Then slowly he framed the words 'Sherlock Holmes', although he made no sound.

'Yes,' said Holmes eagerly. 'And you remember the professor too. Your master.'

Like an eerie whisper, the word 'Moriarty' escaped from Moran's mouth.

'Yes, yes: Moriarty. We need to find him. We need to help him. Professor Moriarty needs our help.'

Moran's brow creased. 'Help?' he said, his voice stronger now.

'Yes, yes, the professor needs our help.'

Moran shook his head in bewilderment.

'We need to reach him. To warn him of danger.'

Suddenly, Moran's eyes opened wide and his whole frame stiffened. 'Dead. The professor is dead,' he said, his voice full of anguish.

'No, no. He is not dead. He survived. He did not drown at Reichenbach. He escaped. He is alive.'

Moran listened to Holmes's words with a puckered brow and after a pause, he grabbed hold of my friend's sleeve. 'Alive? The professor...?'

'Yes. He is alive and we need to reach him. He is in danger. We need to warn him.'

'Alive...' His jaw dropped and saliva collected at the corner of his mouth.

'Yes,' affirmed Holmes again, nodding vigorously and gently shaking Moran's arms. 'We must reach him to protect him. You want to protect your master, don't you? The professor?'

'He is alive? The professor?' The shoulders slumped once more and the eyes misted with tears.

'Yes, Colonel Moran.'

'Colonel Moran?' His features quivered, the forehead creasing and uncreasing with consternation. 'Yes... I am Colonel Sebastian Moran,' he said at length, the old tortured face suddenly regaining some of its life and a smile slowly materialising.

I knew that Moran was a black-hearted villain who, amongst many of his dark deeds, had plotted the assassination of my friend Sherlock Holmes, but I could not help feeling sorry for him now, a shattered wreck of a man who barely remembered who he was. With careful prompting, Holmes was erasing some of the fog that had befuddled his memory, but I think we both knew that any awareness of reality he was able to achieve would be tenuous and short-lived. In the end, this would be for the best. He would spend the rest of his days in this terrible place in a featureless cell unable to communicate with anyone on an intelligent level. Ironically, it would be best that he was left in a state of ignorance.

'Colonel Moran, we have to get news to the professor and we need your help – your help to save him from harm.'

'Help for the professor? Of course.'

'Where is the professor's headquarters? Where is he hiding out?'

Moran's head sank on to his chest once more and he closed his eyes in an attempt to think, a process that was now alien to him.

'Where was his secret place? Where in London?' prompted Holmes gently.

Moran uttered a strange groan and shook his head. 'I don't know,' he said. 'I can't... I can't remember.'

'You must,' snapped Holmes. 'Think. Where did you go to see the professor? Where did you meet him? Picture the place. Imagine it.'

Moran squirmed in his chair and screwed his eyes shut in an attempt to obey Holmes's instructions. The three of us stood and watched as this sad creature, uttering various inarticulate whimpers, tried desperately to summon up images from his past. After a few minutes, he slumped back in the chair, his eyes opening slowly, staring blankly ahead.

'It's no good,' said Beaumont smugly. 'He's too far gone. He's not able to help you.' He seemed almost pleased that this was the case.

Holmes ignored him and patted Moran gently on the shoulder. 'Well you tried, didn't you, Moran.'

At the mention of his name, the tired eyes flickered erratically.

'It was by the river,' he said softly. 'Near the big bridge.'

'Tower Bridge,' I said.

Moran mouthed the words and gave a slight nod. 'Two lions. Golden lions.'

'Where are they? Where are the lions?' asked Holmes gently.

'Above. The lions are above. Before you go below... below to the professor. You go deep.'

'Where exactly is this?' I asked, leaning forward.

'By the river. Near the big bridge,' Moran repeated, now in a sing-song voice. He smiled and added, 'Beneath the golden lions and under to see the professor... the professor. I am Colonel Sebastian Moran.' He giggled and turned his head away.

'What is the address?' asked Holmes urgently, but there was no response. The light that had flickered uncertainly within Moran's eyes had gone and the dazed automaton had returned.

My friend pursed his lips and cast me a glance. 'I believe that we have squeezed the orange dry.'

'I told you you'd get nothing,' sneered Beaumont, placing Moran's cap back on his head, the flap hiding his features once more.

'On the contrary,' asserted Holmes, 'we got more than I'd hoped.'

Beaumont laughed. 'Well, if you're able to make anything out of that rubbishy rigmarole that 142 came out with, you're a better man than I am.'

Holmes did not reply, but merely gave Beaumont a brief smile along with a raise of his eyebrows.

'Do you really think you can make use of the mumblings that Moran made?' I asked earnestly as our cab rattled away from Reading Gaol towards the station.

'You seem to have as little faith in my abilities at that brutish guard,' replied Holmes. 'It is like looking at life through a distorting mirror: perspectives are blurred and out of shape, while nothing seems to fit, but if you tilt your head or arrange your thinking in a certain way, things become recognisable. We have a general location, down by the river, near Tower Bridge and some identifiable landmark of sorts: two golden lions. Not very much to go on, I grant you, but it is *something.*'

'Well,' I said, 'if anyone can make something out of those disparate elements…'

Holmes snorted. 'Watson, my blushes.'

Thirty

'I think he has a fever,' she said with some trepidation.

'Think?' snapped the professor. 'I understood that you were a nurse. Shouldn't you know?'

'I was a nursemaid. I have no medical training, but it is obvious that he has a temperature and is in some discomfort.'

Moriarty moved his wheelchair nearer the bed and gazed down at the young boy, his reddened visage sheened with a fine mist of perspiration. He observed that the child's breathing was even but very shallow. No doubt his condition was a reaction to the upset he had endured in the last few days. If only the brat could have held out a little longer. It looked very much now as though he would need specialised medical treatment. This complicated matters. He couldn't have the boy dying on him before he got his hands on the ransom – just in case he was needed. It was so very annoying. Despite all his meticulous planning, the boy's health was the one thing he could not control.

'See if you can waken the boy and give him some sustenance –

soup maybe. That may rally him. In the meantime I will arrange for a doctor to see to him.'

Without another word, Moriarty swung the wheelchair around and glided towards the door. He travelled along a narrow corridor into a large open room, his office-cum-sitting room, the heart of his underground headquarters. A fire burned brightly in the hearth and the gas lamps graced the chamber with a pleasant amber light. Dominic Gaunt was seated in an armchair by the fireside, a glass of brandy in one hand and a notebook in the other.

'I am sorry to interrupt your period of relaxation and refreshment,' said Moriarty with gentle sarcasm, as he manoeuvred his way towards Gaunt, 'but I have an errand for you.'

Gaunt winced slightly at the use of the word 'errand' as though Moriarty were indirectly placing him firmly in the role of junior dogsbody rather than a senior partner in this venture. In fact now that Jasper Coates was gone, he was the only senior partner and as such he felt that he should be regarded with more respect.

'We have a little problem,' Moriarty was saying. 'Our young charge has taken it upon himself to fall ill at this crucial juncture.'

'How ill?'

Moriarty shrugged. 'That is beyond my realms of expertise and therefore we require the services of a doctor to diagnose the trouble and treat it.'

'A doctor?'

'Indeed, a qualified member of the medical profession,' noted Moriarty with ironic brittleness. Whenever his plans were disarranged in any way, his patience with other mortals was at its weakest and his natural traits of sarcasm and cruelty easily rose to the surface.

'Do you have anyone in mind?'

'There is no one still alive who has provided services for me before. We shall have to choose someone new, snatch a medic at random. Of course, once on these premises, I will not allow them to leave. I will leave it up to you. Just be sure to get someone who has experience with children and have them here within the hour. Make sure that you arrive unseen.'

Gaunt smiled as a thought struck him. 'It would be a delicious irony to scoop up Dr Watson to do our bidding.'

Moriarty did not return the smile. 'Eradicate that notion from your mind immediately, Mr Gaunt. Matters are delicate and critical enough as they are without attempting to complicate them by involving Watson.'

Gaunt shrugged. 'It was just an idea.'

'And a bad one. Dragging Watson here would inevitably bring Sherlock Holmes closer to our table. Do not underestimate that man, Mr Gaunt. Holmes is a genius and is best kept at arm's length. I above all others should know.' He tapped the side of his wheelchair with irritation. 'Holmes is already breathing down our necks and I do not want to provide him with more evidence and impetus by capturing Watson again. Look what happened last time.'

Gaunt's smile disappeared. 'I take your point.'

'Good. Now there is no time to lose. You know what you have to do.'

'Yes, Professor.' Gaunt, aware that he was being dismissed, finished his drink and left the room.

Moriarty smiled to himself. He liked Gaunt, but the young man wasn't yet fully acquainted with the professor's ways or cognisant of the real role he played in Moriarty's scheme of things. Gaunt thought highly of himself and overestimated his own importance. But he would learn. Oh, yes, he would learn. Failure to do so would bring misfortune upon his head.

The smile still wreathing his shattered features, Moriarty moved over to his desk and poured himself a brandy. He drank it slowly, allowing the liquid to roll gently on his tongue and then burn the back of his throat. That's how he liked life: warm pleasure, mixed with a little pain.

'I am afraid your brother is not at home,' said Mrs Hudson as she stood in the hallway of 221B Baker Street, staring up at the towering form of Mycroft Holmes, his features darkened with a mixture of frustration and annoyance. 'He left some time ago with Dr Watson.'

'And I suppose he gave you no indication as to where he was going or when he would return?' he asked coolly.

Mrs Hudson shook her head and smiled indulgently. 'Oh, no. He never does that. Why should he? I have got used to his ways over the years and expect him when I see him. But, of course, you'll know that, being his brother.'

'Oh, yes, I know that. I am fully aware of how unpredictable… and uncommunicative he is. Thank you, ma'am. If, by some miracle, he returns would you ask him to get in touch with me urgently?'

'Of course.'

Mycroft gave the demure lady a stiff bow and left. As he climbed into the waiting carriage, he offered up a little prayer, hoping that Sherlock was actually on the case and making headway. He knew in his heart of hearts that despite all the resources at his command, his brother was the only hope of preventing a national disaster.

* * *

'Dr Murray has finished surgery for the day. Would you like me to book you an appointment for tomorrow?' said the lady with the tight bun and silver-rimmed glasses in a business-like monotone.

Gaunt gave her a stern smile. 'No, I need to see him now. This is an emergency.' He strode past her desk and opened the door marked 'Surgery' and entered.

Dr Graham Murray was writing up some notes on the patients he had seen that day when the stranger burst in and slammed the door shut.

'What the devil,' muttered Murray, half-rising from his chair.

'I need you to come with me now to attend to a sick child,' said the man.

'Who are you?'

'That is of no consequence. You must come with me.'

'I am afraid the surgery is closed for the day. I am not free…'

With a snarl of irritation, Gaunt stepped forward and thrust Murray back into his chair. 'You will do as I say.'

The doctor's eyes widened with surprise and then anger. 'Must I? I think not. If you do not leave my surgery now I will call the police.'

Gaunt removed a pistol from his pocket. 'That would not be a wise move.'

At the sight of the gun, the colour drained from Dr Murray's face. 'Are you mad?' he croaked.

'Collect your things. We are leaving. There is an ailing child who needs your attention. You are a doctor, aren't you? Isn't it your duty to minister to the sick?'

'I do so, but not under duress,' replied Murray, his gaze fixed on the gun the stranger was pointing directly at him.

'You are in no danger as long as you do as you are told. All I am asking of you is to come with me and alleviate a child's suffering. That is not too much to ask, is it?'

Thirty-One

Dr Watson's Journal

Evening was drawing in fast as we reached the north side of the river. Holmes seemed confident that it was upon this particular stretch by Tower Bridge that we would find what we were looking for: Moriarty's lair. We had travelled back from Reading by train and at Paddington station hired a cab to take us to the bridge.

'It will be like looking for a needle in a haystack,' I observed as we stepped from the cab.

'Really, Watson, as a writer of some accomplishment you must avoid using clichés.'

'In some cases, they make their point very succinctly,' I replied tartly.

'Well, it is a fairly well-conceived haystack.' He tapped his temple with his left forefinger. 'You are well aware that I have committed the geographical features and street names of London to memory. No detective of any merit can hope to operate in this metropolis without having a thorough knowledge of its buildings, thoroughfares and byways.'

I knew this to be true. Many was the time that Holmes and I had travelled by cab and so finely attuned was he to the layout of the city that he was able to tell me which particular street we were travelling down without looking out of the window.

'I happen to know there are great stretches of derelict warehouses off Saint Katharine's Way, just a short distance from the bridge towards Wapping. They are the sort of anonymous properties in which a major rat may make his nest. It is somewhere to start at least.'

I nodded without comment. I was still picturing that dull needle lodged in an impenetrable haystack.

We made our way down to the river and to Iron Gate where Tower Bridge stood. It is a magnificent structure, a monument to British engineering and planning. I had been in the crowd a year earlier to watch the Prince of Wales officially open it. Its monumental bulk still remained impressive now, looming darkly above us against the twilight sky.

'It is superb, isn't it, Holmes?' I said, pausing to gaze at the structure.

'Yes, yes,' he responded, somewhat impatiently, 'but we haven't time to behave like tourists. Come along.'

We moved along the embankment for a while and then turned left down a side street into the hinterland that lay north of the river. My comment about a needle in a haystack came back to me once more – and then we had a remarkable stroke of luck. At the far end of one street we observed a hansom cab draw up and two men emerge. As they did so, Holmes pulled me into a doorway.

'By all that's wonderful...' he exclaimed. 'Look who we have here.'

I peered at the two figures and felt the same thrill of excitement exhibited by my companion. Despite the gathering gloom I was able to discern that one of the two men was none other than our old friend, Inspector Dominic Gaunt. The other man, who was a stranger to me, was carrying a medical bag.

Holmes and I exchanged glances. Fortune was indeed smiling on us at last.

Gaunt dismissed the cab and grabbed his companion firmly by the arm. The two men began walking away from us towards the corner of the street.

'Quick, we must not lose them,' cried Holmes, as the pair disappeared from our view.

We hurried down the street, pausing at the corner while Holmes peered cautiously around it. He gave a muted expression of despair.

'They've gone,' he groaned.

We turned into the empty thoroughfare with dismay. They were nowhere to be seen. The street was empty apart from a blind beggar and his dog tapping his way along. It was as though the two men had disappeared into thin air.

Holmes gave a strange little chuckle. 'Well,' he said, 'they cannot have gone far, can they? Surely we can seek them out again.'

I was not convinced as I gazed at the row of buildings, derelict and deserted warehouses, each blank and shabby façade giving no clues as to what lay inside. It could take us hours, days even to search these properties.

Holmes began walking down the street giving each of the premises a close inspection along with the pavement beneath our feet. I followed in his wake and then suddenly he stopped, his whole body stiffening, and once again he gave his strange chuckle.

'Look, Watson, by all that's wonderful.' He raised his cane and pointed to a nearby doorway. Above the shabby door, covered in grime, were the carved forms of two lions. Beneath them was a small sign in faded script: 'Leonine Chambers'.

'Remember what Moran said in his ramblings about golden lions. It is too much to be a coincidence. This must be the entrance to Moriarty's lair.'

I nodded enthusiastically. I did not doubt that my friend was correct.

Without hesitation, he approached the door and tried the handle. It was locked. 'This lock should not provide much of a hindrance,' he observed, extracting the small burglar's pouch from his overcoat. I glanced up and down the street as Holmes set to work on the lock. There was no one about and already night was providing a sufficient cloak to mask our activities.

Within a few minutes Holmes had succeeded in his task. He turned the handle and the door swung open. He pulled it to again and turned to me.

'This is where we part company, Watson.'

'What!' I exclaimed, completely baffled by this announcement.

'I must tackle Moriarty alone.'

'But he is not alone. There is at least Gaunt and the fellow we saw with him.'

'Nonetheless, this is my challenge, not yours. You have other duties that are essential to the success of our mission.'

'Really,' I said somewhat indignantly.

'This is obviously Moriarty's hideout – and it is probably where he is keeping the boy. Both Mycroft and Scotland Yard need to be alerted to this fact. It is up to you to inform them while I beard our notorious lion in his den.'

'Why don't we both go to Scotland Yard?' I said. 'Now you have located Moriarty's place, it would be much safer to storm the place with a pack of armed constables.'

'Safer for whom? Not the boy. This has to be handled delicately. It is time that Moriarty and I face each other once again. I have to be trusted in this matter.'

I knew in my heart of hearts that my friend was right, but I was severely disappointed to be dismissed and sent on an errand rather than be at what I supposed would be the climax of the case. Reluctant as I was to allow Sherlock Holmes to enter that crumbling old warehouse on his own, I knew that any argument I put forward would be ignored. I could see the cold hard determination in those steely grey eyes, which prevented me from raising any objection to his wishes.

'Very well,' I said quietly.

'Good man.' He pulled open the door again and moved to step inside.

I placed my hand on his shoulder. 'For heaven's sake, take care,' I said.

'Of course,' he replied, before stepping into the darkness. With an eerie creak, the door shut behind him.

I wasted no time and headed back towards the main road at a quick pace. I knew that time was of the essence. I was not happy at the thought of Holmes alone in Moriarty's lair and the sooner that I secured help the better.

It was quite dark now and the street was illuminated by only a couple of gas lamps. As I reached the corner, a figure emerged from the shadows. My heart skipped a beat, but I did not lessen my pace. The figure stepped in front of me blocking my way and I saw that it was the blind beggar we had seen earlier. He held out his hand as though proffering his begging cup, but instead of a cup, he held a revolver.

'Stop where you are, Dr Watson,' he said in a gruff but educated voice. 'Do exactly as I tell you or I will be forced to kill you. Those were my orders. And, believe me, I always obey my orders.'

Thirty-Two

As the large door closed behind Sherlock Holmes with a rather chilling finality, he was plunged into near darkness. There were faint glimmerings of light at the far end of the chamber, but they provided scant illumination. The acrid smell of damp and decay assailed his nostrils and he was conscious of the scuffles and rustlings of unseen rats as they scurried fitfully in the gloom. He cursed himself for not bringing a dark lantern and resigned himself to stand fast while his eyes accustomed themselves to the gloom. Gradually faint shadows strengthened in the darkness and he was able to formulate a sketchy image of his surroundings. Slowly, using his cane as a blind man would, he began to move forward towards the light at the far end of the chamber, tapping the end of his stick gently in order to avoid any obstacle in his way. There were several mainly empty wicker baskets, remnants of the days when this was a trading warehouse. As he pushed one of these baskets to one side, a creature scuttled over his hand. He gave a sharp intake of breath in surprise, but made no other sound. As he neared the faint glow of light, he could see that it was a solitary oil lamp hanging from a beam. Below it was another door. This one appeared new and comparatively modern and was obviously a more recent addition, as was, Holmes was now able to observe, the wall into which it was fixed. Obviously some bespoke alterations had been made to these decrepit quarters by its new master.

Slipping his cane under his arm, he withdrew his revolver before trying the door. This time the door swung open easily and he found himself in a small illuminated chamber. Before him was a strange gated cage contraption, which Holmes deduced was a lift shaft. A mechanism in which visitors and indeed the professor himself would be transferred to the heart of this structure: the professor's secret headquarters. Of course, he told himself, this was not just some sophisticated addition: it was a necessary device. The wheelchair-bound Moriarty would certainly not be able to use stairs.

Slowly Holmes pulled back the gate and looked down the shaft, observing that the lift was at the bottom of its trajectory. Obviously it had been used by Gaunt and his companion. Holmes gazed at the glimmering lights at the bottom where he could discern the top of the lift cage. He gauged that the drop was some twenty feet. Slipping his revolver into his trouser pocket and discarding his cane, he leaned out into the gloom and grasped the thick wire that operated the lift. It was cold and caked in oil. Securing what he hoped would be a strong enough grip, he allowed his body to sway outwards, his legs clamping themselves around the wire. The combination of his weight and the lubrication of the oil allowed him to slide slowly and silently down.

Within less than a minute, Holmes had landed gently on the roof of the lift. He steadied himself and allowed a few seconds to catch his breath before discarding his overcoat, which was now heavily smeared with oil. In the dim light, he allowed his fingers to explore the top of the lift until they found what he was looking for: the trap built into all such structures to allow engineers access to the workings above. He lifted the rectangular piece of metal and slid it to one side, revealing an aperture large enough for him to pass through and drop down into the body of the lift. He landed softly and quickly took note of his surroundings. Beyond the cage door of the lift he observed a brightly lit vestibule with a door which led, he had no doubt, into the main part of these secret quarters.

There were times in his career when Sherlock Holmes knew that he had to dispense with caution in order to advance the case. Risks, he concurred, were after all part of his trade and if he was not prepared to take them, success would inevitably elude him. But of course he was also cognisant of the fact that in taking a risk, one could place oneself in great danger and risk failure. Here he was in the heart of the domain of his old archenemy, a creature he had long thought dead, but who had risen from the ashes of his own supposed demise to threaten the security of the country. He had to grasp the nettle and step through the door before him.

Gripping his revolver firmly, he turned the handle.

The chamber in which Sherlock Holmes found himself was harshly illuminated, throwing certain sections of the chamber into inky shadow. The room was richly furnished, rather like, he thought, a well-appointed drawing room in a London mansion. The walls were panelled and adorned with paintings. A chandelier hung incongruously from the wooden rafters. There were several armchairs, a chaise longue and a large ornate desk. A fire burnt in a large stone fireplace at one end of the room.

At first glance the room appeared to be empty and for a split second Holmes relaxed his defences, but then the air was filled with a strange whirring noise and, as though materialising from the dark shadows in the corner of the room, Professor Moriarty appeared before him. He glided forward in his motorised wheelchair to within six feet of Sherlock Holmes.

'So, we meet again, Mr Holmes,' he said in a strange croaky voice. 'Strangely, this encounter is not a surprise to either of us.'

'Perhaps not, although until recently I assumed the only time it was likely that our paths would cross would be in the great hereafter – but perhaps not even then, you having gone to the other place.'

Moriarty chuckled mirthlessly. 'An amusing concept.'

'I have come for the child,' said Holmes, taking a step closer to the professor, raising his gun so that it was aimed at his heart.

Moriarty chuckled again. 'Ever the dashing hero, full of melodramatics, eh, Holmes?' Slowly he pulled back the rug that was lying over his knees to reveal a shotgun. He aimed it in Holmes's direction. 'This has tremendous power and should I pull the trigger the impact would no doubt fling you back against the wall, leaving a substantial hole in your midriff. While your little pistol would have little effect on a man wearing a bulletproof armour breastplate – a very special one of my own design based on the Zeglen principle. You really should have one – especially in your line of business. You never know when someone might take a pot shot at you, eh?' The smile on Moriarty's face faded as he raised the shotgun.

'A bulletproof breastplate does not protect *all* vulnerable areas,' observed Holmes tartly, his hand not wavering in the least.

'Oh, do let's be civil about this, Holmes. You know as well as I do that you will not get out of here alive. You will not be surprised to learn that I fully expected that you would land up here – washed ashore like an unwanted piece of driftwood. Your usual curiosity and brilliance guaranteed that. Thus I was prepared for such an eventuality and indeed allowed you to make your way down here unhindered. You do not think for a moment that this place is not guarded twenty-four hours by my trusted employees. Under normal circumstances, you would have been eliminated once you had entered the building above, but I was... how shall I say... intrigued to meet you once more – for a final time. You are often in my thoughts – the man who robbed me of my health and my ability to walk.'

'Ah, but it was you who hounded me, if you remember, Professor. You who hounded me all the way across Europe to the Reichenbach Falls. And it was Fate that decreed that I should survive and you...'

'Fate is such an intangible thing. I need something... someone more concrete to blame.'

'So it is revenge that you seek.'

Moriarty emitted a theatrical laugh. 'Oh, yes, it is revenge. My plans always involved that element. I knew full well that my audacious scheme – you will allow me the term audacious, I hope – would inevitably lure you into my machinations. If the Temples did not apply to you for help, then your brother would inevitably drag you into the net.'

'I am flattered that I should have been such an important consideration in your plans.'

'How could you not? For years you were a thorn in my flesh, upsetting my operations, foiling my ventures – but since Reichenbach ... since Reichenbach...' For a moment the eyes lost their fire and darkened as his left hand caressed the rim of the wheel of the mechanised chair while his mouth tightened. And then in an instant, Moriarty had regained his composure and his *savoir faire* once again.

'Since Reichenbach your destruction has been my most fervent wish and most of my energies have been channelled to that end. In my current venture it pleasured me to think that I was hitting several targets with one arrow: upsetting the British government and the monarchy, accruing a large fortune and having a final chat with my old friend Sherlock Holmes before ending his life.'

Moriarty's hands shook slightly with emotion as he raised the shotgun a little higher. Just as it seemed that he was about to pull the trigger, he was distracted by a strange whistling sound that emanated from a speaking tube on his desk. With a dextrous movement, Moriarty propelled the wheelchair backwards so that it reached the desk, while keeping the weapon trained on Holmes. He lifted up the speaking tube from its cradle and listened. As he did so his mouth broadened into a wide malevolent grin.

'Excellent. Bring him down.'

His grin remained as he replaced the tube on its cradle.

Holmes moved closer to the desk, still pointing the gun at Moriarty. 'What do you intend to do with the child?'

'Do with him? What do you think I am going to do with him? The boy is my safeguard. He will remain with me for the time being. I will have great pleasure in reading him your obituary in the newspapers. Your second. I do hope the press do you justice – but alas, you know how unreliable they are.'

'Where is he now?'

Moriarty's head turned slightly. It was only an infinitesimal movement before he checked himself, but Holmes observed it. Moriarty's automatic reaction had informed him that the boy was situated somewhere behind the large bookcase against the wall. No doubt this was concealing a doorway to another part of Moriarty's quarters. There was nothing that Holmes could do about it now, but he regarded it as useful information nonetheless.

'The whereabouts of the boy are of no consequence to you now,' said Moriarty, taking two glasses from the silver tray on his desk and placing them in the centre. 'Call me sentimental, Sherlock Holmes, but I have a whim to take a final drink with you. We have gazed at each other for some time across the great divide that separates us and yet we share some strange kind of bond. We are both masters of our profession, you and I; meticulous, brilliant and resourceful. It is these qualities that almost make us brothers.'

'For a mathematician, you are somewhat fanciful,' said Holmes, his manner relaxed, belying his inner tensions. He knew that he had to keep Moriarty talking. The longer he distracted him in this fashion, the more it allowed time for Watson to reach Scotland Yard. He had no concerns for his own safety, just as long as the boy was rescued and Moriarty was captured. 'There is nothing that binds us,' he continued. 'Far from it. We are poles apart in outlook, morality and vision. Your success in the world is only as a criminal preying on the weak and the good, using corrupt, mentally inferior individuals as minions to carry out your nefarious plans for personal gain and to increase your sense of power over the innocent and unsuspecting.'

'Bravo, Holmes. How eloquent.'

'The criminal mind such as yours has a distorted view of the world and concepts. Your triumphs are mean and degraded. There is no glory in what you do. In fact, Professor Moriarty, nothing separates you from the thug who knocks over an old lady and snatches her purse for his gin money. When the history of the world is written, you will only be regarded as a worm.'

The insouciant smile that had lingered on Moriarty's lips faded and his body stiffened. It was clear to Holmes that his words had, as he intended, hit home and irritated the professor. For some moments he appeared to be lost for words, unsure how to respond to the detective's barbs. He opened his mouth to say something, but as he did so the speaking tube on his desk made the strange whistling sound again. Moriarty grabbed it and listened. The smile returned.

'Excellent,' he said. 'Bring him in.'

The door through which Holmes had entered swung open and two men entered. One of them Holmes recognised as the beggar they had passed on their way to Leonine Chambers. The other was Watson.

Thirty-Three

In a room close by, Dr Graham Murray was leaning over the bed in which William Temple was lying. The doctor was shaking his head ruefully. 'There is nothing I can do to help the boy. He needs hospital treatment. His condition has gone beyond the powers of my pills and tinctures.'

Gaunt, who stood some distance away, snarled in anger. 'You are a doctor. Treat him!'

Murray faced his aggressor fearlessly. 'You can shout all you want at me and wave that gun in my direction, but it will not help to cure this child. Yes, as you state, I am a doctor and as such do you think I would renege on my Hippocratic Oath and refrain from helping someone who was ill if it were within my power? This boy has a fever and is slipping into a coma. He needs specialised treatment, and oxygen. I am only a general practitioner.'

Gaunt's eyes twitched anxiously, his fury dissipating. Murray could see that the man was perplexed and unsure what to do. Perhaps now was the time to try and take this matter into his own hands...

211

Thirty-Four

From Dr Watson's Journal

With his pistol pressed firmly in my back, I was led by the beggar into the building that Holmes had entered less than fifteen minutes earlier. Once inside I was taken into a side room, the entrance of which was disguised by cunningly arranged fallen rafters and large drapes of sacking. Here, my captor lit an oil lamp to reveal a small cabinet on the wall from which he produced a speaking tube, similar to those used aboard ships. He spoke to someone at the other end, gleefully announcing my capture.

Replacing the contraption, he grinned broadly at me. 'The boss wants to see you. You'll enjoy that.' He gurgled unpleasantly as he prodded me with the gun once more.

We moved from this cramped chamber back into the main body of the building. I was led in the gloom towards the far end of the property and through another door into a vestibule where to my surprise there was a lift contraption. He pressed one of the buttons on the wall, and with a muted whirring and clanking sound the lift cage eventually hove into view.

'Nice little thing, ain't it?' said the beggar, pulling back the sliding cage door. 'In you go, Doctor.'

With a juddering motion, the lift began to descend.

'I reckon that'll be your last journey. Hope you enjoyed it,' he grinned, as we stepped from the lift. 'Now through that door.'

The room I found myself in was large and surprisingly well appointed. It was like encountering a lush oasis in the barren sands of the desert. I was conscious of the warmth provided by a blazing fire, but what immediately caught my attention and rooted me to the spot was the sight of the two individuals facing each other by a large desk. One was in a wheelchair brandishing a large shotgun. The other, standing close to him, was Sherlock Holmes.

The man in the wheelchair beckoned to me. 'Ah, do come in, Doctor Watson. We meet at last. Let me introduce myself,' he said with an easy smile.

'I know who and what you are,' I replied coldly, as I tried to conceal the shock I felt at finally seeing the ghost of the arch criminal before me. My heart thudded in my breast.

'I could say the same of you. But let us not bandy words about now. Come forward and take a drink with me and your erstwhile companion Holmes here.'

I moved forward, glancing at Holmes, who raised his eyebrows in query. I knew what he was thinking, what he wanted to know: had I managed to summon help? I gave a brief shake of the head. I saw my friend's lips tighten in disappointment.

'Come, Holmes, be sociable and pour your partner a drink.'

Holmes hesitated and Moriarty raised his shotgun a fraction. 'I insist,' he said, the voice suddenly full of undisguised menace.

Slowly and with reluctance Holmes did as he was bidden.

'That's better,' said Moriarty and then turned his attention to the beggar who was hovering by the door. 'That will be all, Crowther. Back to your post. And good work.'

The beggar grinned. 'Thank you, sir,' he said before leaving.

'Now it's just the three of us. How cosy.'

'What do you intend to do?' I asked.

'Do take your drink, Watson. What do I intend to do? Well, I think you know the answer to that. As I was just explaining to Holmes before you arrived, the successful completion of my plan will be crowned by the destruction of your friend here… what did you once call him, "the best and wisest man I have ever known"? And, of course you will be joining him in that bourne from which no traveller returns, so I'm afraid you will not be around to write an overblown obituary for him this time or even record his last words.' With a sudden swivel of the head he turned to Holmes. 'In fact, do you have any last words, Mr Holmes, before I pull the trigger?'

'Actions speak louder than words,' snapped Holmes and with a quick movement fired his pistol at Moriarty's legs while at the same time throwing his drink into the villain's face.

The professor cried out in pain, but such was his steel that he was only momentarily distracted and he fired the shotgun at Holmes, but he, by now, was swiftly on the move and the shot missed him by inches. Moriarty turned his attention to me and fired in my direction, but his reactions were slower than mine and I dropped to the floor, safely missing the round that flew over my head.

Holmes rushed forward and with great force snatched the gun from Moriarty's grasp. 'No time to reload now, Professor,' he said, hurling the gun to the other end of the room. 'Watson, who has a liking for clichés, will no doubt pen the one about tables being turned when he comes to write an account of this meeting.'

Moriarty rubbed his wounded leg but kept his composure.

Then suddenly there was the sound of a shot and a muffled cry from somewhere else in the building. We followed Moriarty's gaze to a bookcase on the far wall. Holmes raced towards it and within seconds I saw that he was able to pull the whole structure back like a large door. 'You keep an eye on our friend, here, Watson, while I investigate,' he cried as he disappeared down the dimly lighted corridor beyond.

I turned to face the professor just in time for me to see him extract a small revolver from his inside pocket. 'An old maxim of mine: never rely on one weapon. But no time for chit-chat now, Watson,' he said, aiming the gun at me and firing.

Thirty-Five

Holmes made his way down a narrow corridor, along which were three doors. He tried the first, which revealed a large unoccupied bedroom with a four-poster bed. He assumed that this must be Moriarty's private quarters. As he approached the second room, he heard two more shots ring out from the chamber where he had just left Watson and Moriarty. In a split second, his mind reviewed several possible scenarios. His body trembled with indecision. Should he return to the room and investigate? Or should he continue his search? Rarely had the detective been faced with such a dilemma. It might well be that Watson needed his help, or worse still that it was too late.

However, Fate took the decision from him, for the door of the second room opened suddenly and Dominic Gaunt appeared in the aperture, his face damp with sweat and his eyes wild and darting. He staggered into the corridor and on seeing Holmes he gave a raw guttural cry. He raised a pistol, but with frenetic speed Holmes leapt forward and knocked the weapon from his hand before bringing his fist into forceful contact with Gaunt's chin. The man staggered backwards, but managed to maintain his equilibrium. The blow seemed to focus his mind and galvanise his energies all the more. He gave a rasping cry and rushed at Holmes, thrusting him against the wall. The two men struggled, each one approaching the task in a different fashion. Gaunt was frantic, his mind full of anger and disappointment. His fury increased his strength, which momentarily gave him an advantage over Holmes who, while being calmer and more methodical, lacked the mad passion of his opponent.

As they struggled, the two men crashed to the floor, rolling over entwined in each other's grip. Gaunt wrenched his hands free and grabbed Holmes by the throat and began to throttle the detective. Deftly, Holmes brought his arms up, breaking Gaunt's grip and then with a great effort he managed to heave his assailant sideways. This gave him the freedom to scramble to his feet once more. Gaunt swivelled round into a crouching position, panting heavily, his face gleaming with perspiration. For a few seconds the two men stared at each other, still as statues, uncertain what the other would do next. And then Gaunt launched himself forward, reaching out for his gun, which lay a few yards from him on the floor. With glee he snatched it up and staggered to his feet. Like lightning Holmes reached out and grabbed his wrist before he was able to aim it. Once more the two men wrestled with each other for mastery. Holmes thrust Gaunt against the wall, winding him, and attempted to shake the gun from his grasp by slamming his arm with great force against the woodwork. Gritting his teeth and emitting a deep feral growl, Gaunt pushed hard against his opponent and managed to wrench his arm from Holmes's grip.

Suddenly the gun went off.

Once again both men froze, static figures in the gloomy corridor. And then, Gaunt's eyes widened with a sudden horrid realisation. His lips quivered momentarily as though he was about to say something, but no words emerged. Holmes felt Gaunt's whole frame relax and lose its tension. Gently, he released his hold and took a step back as his opponent's body slid down to the floor. For a moment the eyes remained open, gazing vacantly and then very slowly they closed forever.

Holmes stood for a moment, gaining his breath and composure. He felt no sense of triumph. Killing a man was not a thing to be proud of. He would have much preferred to bring the fellow to justice. It was for the judiciary to pronounce sentence, not him. He was a detective, a solver of crimes – not an executioner.

Mopping his brow, he sent these gloomy thoughts to the back of his mind as he entered the room from which Gaunt had appeared. Once inside, the sight that met his eyes sickened him further. There on the floor was another corpse. That of the man Holmes had glimpsed with Gaunt entering the building. Obviously he was a doctor of some kind: the stethoscope around his neck and the medical bag on the bedside table proclaimed as much. He knelt down and felt the man's pulse just to be certain he was dead. There was no doubt. In turning over the body, he saw the savage wound to the chest. A victim no doubt of Dominic Gaunt. At this sight, he felt a lessening of his own guilt at being responsible for the death of the corrupt policeman.

Rising slowly, he observed the shape under crumpled covers on the bed. He hurried forward and pulled back the blanket to reveal the face of a young boy beneath. It was flushed and still. This innocent little boy was what all the death and violence had been about. This was William Temple – the potential heir to the throne.

Holmes dragged the blankets back further to reveal the little night-gowned figure. He lay very still, curled into a ball.

'My God,' murmured Sherlock Holmes, gazing at the lifeless form, 'we are too late: the boy is dead.'

Thirty-Six

Dr Watson's Journal

Having produced a small pistol from his jacket pocket, Professor Moriarty had leaned forward in his chair and fired two shots in my direction. Instinctively, I dived to the ground in a desperate attempt to avoid the bullets. I managed to do so, but in landing awkwardly I banged the side of my head on the edge of a small marble table. I felt a violent stabbing pain to the temple. In an instant darkness and silence engulfed me.

I was only unconscious for a very short time, but when I dragged myself groggily to my feet, my eyes gradually focusing on my surroundings, I discovered that the room was empty: the professor had gone. No doubt he had assumed that as I had crashed to the ground and remained still, he had been successful in his attempt to kill me. Now my concern was to locate him. Then I heard the whirr of the lift mechanism. Blinking hard to clear my head, I made a move towards the vestibule where the lift was situated. As I did so, I heard another shot. It came from the direction of the door through which Holmes had disappeared. For a moment I hesitated, my brain only slowly returning to normal after the blow to my head. No doubt, I reasoned, Moriarty would have made good his escape by means of the lift. By the time I made my way to the upper floor in pursuit, he would have already fled the building. However, the shot I had just heard might well indicate that Holmes was in trouble and in need of my help.

As swiftly as I could I changed my course and made my way towards the doorway revealed by the moveable bookcase. Passing through into a narrow corridor, I encountered the body of Dominic Gaunt. Kneeling down I took his pulse. The man was dead. A crimson stain spreading across his waistcoat gave evidence as to the cause of death. Gaunt lay across the width of the passageway, his body twisted awkwardly, but his face with the eyes closed looked serene and at peace. It is strange that no matter what paths we take in life, what morals we adhere to, what gods we worship, death homogenises us all.

Stepping over him, I continued down the corridor to where a door stood open. In the lighted room beyond I discovered Holmes, leaning over a huddled form on a bed.

'Holmes!' I cried, my voice hoarse with emotion. 'Thank heavens you're safe.'

He turned to me and gave a tight grin. 'And you too, old fellow. We survive. Unfortunately, I cannot say the same for this poor mite.' He turned his gaze back to the shape on the bed.

I took a step forward and saw that it was a boy – *the* boy. The child we had been searching for since the start of this dark business. We had found him at last.

'I fear we got here too late,' said Holmes softly, running his hand across his brow.

'No!' I gasped in horror and bent over the child. His features were still and the face clammy with sweat. I lifted his limp arm and felt for a pulse. 'No,' I said again, but this time my utterance carried a different meaning. It was not an exclamation of despair, but one of hope. Holmes had been wrong. Faint, like the fragile fluttering of a butterfly, I could feel his pulse.

'This boy is not dead,' I proclaimed. 'There is still life there. It is faint, feeble but with a gentle regularity. The boy is fighting.'

Holmes's eyes widened in surprise. 'Are you sure?'

The butterfly fluttered again.

'I am sure,' I said. 'We need to get this lad to a hospital immediately. If he is to survive he needs specialised treatment.'

'He must survive!'

I nodded and began wrapping the frail creature in a blanket.

'Moriarty?' said Holmes, his voice full of apprehension.

'He has escaped I'm afraid.'

Holmes gave a sharp rasp of frustration. 'He has the luck of the Devil!' he cried. 'Still, we know his plans.'

For a few moments Holmes sunk his head on his chest and closed his eyes. 'Very well,' he announced briskly, his eyes snapping open, shining with excitement. 'I charge you with the task of conveying this poor creature to the hospital.'

'Why certainly but—'

'In the meantime I will alert the authorities as to what has happened. Mycroft should be able to get things moving pretty sharply. At least we can prevent the ransom being paid. The game is not over yet.'

Thirty-Seven

ᦐ

Dr Watson's Journal

Within half an hour of leaving Moriarty's secret headquarters, I was sitting in a corridor of Bart's Hospital waiting anxiously for a report on William Temple's condition. I had taken him to this particular hospital, my old *alma mater*, because I was familiar with its system and I was known there as an 'old boy' and I felt sure that I would be able to obtain immediate attention for the child. This indeed turned out to be the case for only minutes after crossing the threshold, my charge had been whipped away and a portly physician by the name of Maxwell, whom I did not know, assured me he would do his best to save the lad. I knew that I could not have expected a better response. This did not calm my nerves however, for I knew how critical his condition was. As we had travelled by cab, the boy had been cradled in my arms and that sad moist face had shown no real signs of life. It was only that frail pulse that gave any indication that the child was still clinging on to life. In my heart of hearts I feared the worst.

What further increased my distress was the fact that I was now essentially an impotent pawn in this grim and complicated game that Holmes and I were involved in. I had done all I could to help save the child's life – the rest of that particular journey was in other, more experienced hands – and I was no longer able to offer assistance to Holmes in his exertions. Where was he now? I wondered. And where was Moriarty? They were questions that had no satisfactory answer and all I could do was to sit on a hard chair in this lonely hospital corridor waiting in a kind of limbo. For a man of action, as I rather arrogantly considered myself to be, this was a sentence of the harshest torture.

It is at times like this that time seems to slow to a snail's pace. I tried to avoid checking my watch frequently, but failed. The hands on the clock face seemed hardly to move at all, as though the cursed instrument had stopped functioning, and yet it seemed hours since I had arrived at the hospital. Occasionally I rose from the chair and walked up and down the corridor to alleviate my frustrated boredom. There was a constant parade of nurses, orderlies and doctors passing me by, most of whom hardly gave me a glance.

And then at long last, I observed the bulky form of Maxwell appear at the far end of the corridor rather like a mirage. His shape was ill-defined at first, as though I were viewing him through frosted glass. I put this visual anomaly down to my tiredness and anxiety. Clarity gradually reasserted itself as he approached me. My heart sank when I saw the gloomy expression on his face and the beads of perspiration dotting his brow as he sat himself beside me with a heavy sigh.

Thirty-Eight

The carriage bearing the legend 'Thompson's Tinned Meat Products' painted on the side pulled off the main road into a field, as had been instructed. The driver, Arthur Moxon, a sergeant in the Metropolitan Police disguised in scruffy workman's clothing, tensed in readiness for the next and what he assumed would be the most dramatic stage of his journey. All that had been planned for this venture had suddenly been scrapped. His role as a docile delivery man had been changed dramatically at the eleventh hour.

Instinctively Moxon's hand slipped inside his jacket, the fingers clasping around the handle of his pistol. The feel of the cold metal gave him a sense of security and comfort. He had never actually used it while on duty, but he knew that he would need it tonight. He fought hard to quell his nerves while he waited patiently. Gazing out at the darkness before him, he could gradually make out the shapes of three carriages in the far corner of the field and emerging from each of them were several men, around eight in all, moving towards him. Three of them carried lanterns; the others carried rifles and pistols.

'They're on their way,' said Moxon, leaning back so that his voice would carry. In response to this, there was a faint rustling noise in the rear of the vehicle.

By now the group of men had reached the carriage and one man stepped forward from the rest, pointing a rifle at Moxon. 'Step down. We mean you no harm if you behave yourself. Our interest is in the contents of your conveyance. Once we have removed it, we will let you go without harm.'

Slowly, Moxon did as was asked and clambered down from the vehicle on to the wet grass. He moved towards the leader of the group with such confidence that he, surprised at the driver's effrontery, took a step back.

Noting the fleeting sign of apprehension on the man's face, Moxon smiled. 'I should advise you in your own best interests that it would be sensible if you dropped your weapons now,' he said, edging even nearer. 'That way no one will get hurt.'

The leader of the group laughed. 'Well, you're a cocky one, ain't you? You going to take us on single-handed, eh?'

'Not quite,' said Moxon, turning his head to the carriage from which a dozen officers with rifles had emerged silently and stood in readiness.

'What is this?' cried the leader of the group, panic rising in his voice.

'It is a rout,' said Moxon. 'That's what it is. The game is up, gentlemen. You are all under arrest. Do not attempt to run away. If you do, you will be shot. Now, throw down your weapons.'

The officers moved forward, rifles cocked.

'Bugger!' said one of the men as he let his pistol fall to the ground.

* * *

The telephone rang shrilly, breaking an interminable silence. Mycroft snatched it up eagerly. His tense features, sharpened by the table lamp, relaxed and his eyes brightened as he listened to the voice at the other end. 'Excellent!' he cried. 'Excellent!' And he slammed the receiver down with a great sigh of satisfaction. 'It's over, Sherlock. It's over. They've captured Moriarty's men – or the rump of them at least. No doubt some of the minor players will slip through the net, but the main thing is that the danger is past. Thank God you found the child in time. We certainly couldn't have carried out such an operation if the professor still had his hands on the boy.'

'You speak of the child as though he were an object, an item. He is a fragile pawn in this treacherous game and has suffered greatly from his ordeal. While you and your government friends can break open the champagne none of you care whether William Temple is alive or dead.'

'Of course we do, Sherlock. Forgive me if I gave you a different impression. But in the great scheme of things this is a personal tragedy. You must stand back and observe the greater picture. The life of a child, while precious, is nothing compared to the stability of the monarchy and the security of a nation. If we had failed, chaos would have resulted; the country would be turmoil. But, thanks to you, this has been avoided and the plot has been foiled.'

Sherlock Holmes lit a cigarette before responding. 'Indeed, it is true: the plot has been foiled. You have a band of ruffians in custody, but the professor has got away. He is not one of your minor players.'

Mycroft nodded and a sympathetic smile touched his tired

features for a brief moment. 'Moriarty. Yes, I fear so, but I am afraid it is a price I am prepared to pay for the destruction of his plan and the removal of the threat to the British monarchy and the government. In my eyes, all's well that ends well.'

'Not for me,' replied Holmes wearily, stubbing out his cigarette with some force.

In a first-class cabin on the night ferry to Dieppe, Professor James Moriarty was also smoking a cigarette and feeling similarly dismayed. All his careful planning and organisation had in the end come to naught. There was no financial reward and what was perhaps worse, that devil Sherlock Holmes had beaten him again. He gave a deep groan of anger. 'One day,' he muttered, 'one day that man will pay. I will see to it.' With a sudden movement he too stubbed out his cigarette with remarkable violence.

Thirty-Nine

Dr Watson's Journal

Dawn was breaking over the city as I made my way along Baker Street. I was weary and strangely numb as though my tiredness was acting like an anaesthetic. I climbed the seventeen steps slowly and entered our sitting room. I was pleased to see Sherlock Holmes at the breakfast table with a pot of coffee.

'Watson, my dear fellow, I am so very glad to see you,' he said, rising from his chair and advancing towards me. For one moment I thought he was going to embrace me. Instead he helped me off with my coat, ushered me to a chair at the table and poured me a cup of coffee. 'How does the boy?'

'He lives,' I said.

'That is wonderful news.'

'It was touch and go. We nearly lost him, but a brilliant fellow at Bart's managed to pull him through.'

Holmes chuckled. 'Bart's, eh? I thought you'd take the lad there. Your old stamping ground. He will make a full recovery?'

I nodded. 'So I am led to believe. And what of Moriarty and the ransom?'

'I will tell you all over breakfast. I can see that you are in desperate need of some sustenance. I'll ring for Mrs Hudson. And when you have eaten, we shall take ourselves off to Bart's and visit the little invalid.'

It was mid-morning by the time we reached the hospital. I led the way to the room where I had last seen William only to find it empty and the bed stripped of its linen.

'He's been moved,' I cried, somewhat puzzled. 'Where to, I wonder?'

'I am afraid you will never know that.' The voice came from the doorway and we turned and saw the imposing figure of Mycroft Holmes.

'What have you done with William Temple?' asked Holmes brusquely.

'Tut, tut, dear boy,' replied his brother silkily, 'you don't expect me to tell you that.'

'What on earth's going on here?' I asked, making no attempt to keep the anger from my voice.

'William Temple has been removed to a safe place where he will be cared for appropriately.'

'What do you mean, "appropriately"?'

'He means in secret,' said Holmes.

'Indeed,' agreed Mycroft. 'The boy is still a living threat to the monarchy. There may be other villains who share the same ideas as Professor Moriarty. We have to protect ourselves from them.'

'This is monstrous,' I cried.

'It is better than the alternative. He must be removed from all danger for his own sake as well as ours.'

'Is he to live the life of a hermit?'

Mycroft gave me a half-smile and shook his head. 'Not quite, but he will be... monitored. I am sure you understand, Sherlock.'

'I understand, but I do not condone. What of the poor parents – the Temples? Are they never to see their son again?'

'I fear not. You must remember that he was not their son; that is the problem. I am sure time will heal their wounds.'

'Glibly said, brother.'

My anger and dismay had robbed me of words and I strode from the room, desperately needing some fresh air. As I stood on the steps of that great hospital, I was joined some minutes later by Holmes, who laid a hand on my shoulder. 'I know how you feel, old boy. I agree it is harsh, but perhaps it is for the best.'

'The best for whom?'

'I am not sure. Only time will reveal the answer to that conundrum. Ah, it has been a most disturbing affair. At the conclusion, Mycroft is happy, the government is happy, but for the rest of us...'

There is little left to tell. Sadly the Temples never recovered from the loss of their precious child. Although he was not of their own flesh and blood they perhaps loved him all the more because of this. The pain they endured as a result of this brutal separation was great. Mrs Temple in particular felt his absence the most and her health declined rapidly. It would seem that she had little energy or enthusiasm to aid her own recovery. Within three years of the events I have just recounted, the lady died. In deep grief Temple moved away from London and I lost track of him.

Holmes too sank into a depression for several months following the affair. He did not speak of his feelings to me – he rarely did – but I could see that the unfortunate circumstances surrounding the child and the cruel fate suffered by the Temples affected him greatly. However I am also sure that the greatest reason for his malaise was the knowledge that Professor Moriarty was alive and free. For years my friend had been secure in the belief that he had rid the world of this wicked criminal mastermind and now he had to accept the terrible truth that this was not so. He saw it as his great failure – a failure allied to a threat. Now he could never be sure when the dark spectre of Professor James Moriarty would come back to haunt him again.

About the Author

D avid Stuart Davies is a renowned expert on the Great Detective. He is the author of three 'Further Adventures' titles, *The Devil's Promise*, *The Veiled Detective* and *The Scroll of the Dead* for Titan Books, as well as numerous other Sherlock Holmes novels, and the hit plays *Sherlock Holmes: The Last Act* and *Sherlock Holmes: The Death and Life*. He was editor of *Sherlock Holmes: The Detective Magazine*.

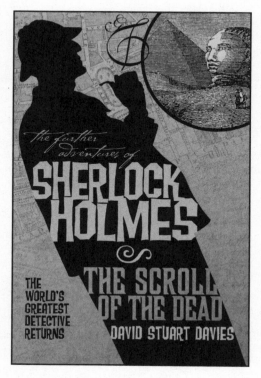

THE FURTHER ADVENTURES
OF SHERLOCK HOLMES

THE SCROLL OF THE DEAD

David Stuart Davies

In this fast-paced adventure, Sherlock Holmes attends a séance to unmask an impostor posing as a medium. His foe, Sebastian Melmoth, is a man hell-bent on discovering a mysterious Egyptian papyrus that may hold the key to immortality. It is up to Holmes and Watson to use their deductive skills to stop him or face disaster.

ISBN: 9781848564930

AVAILABLE NOW!

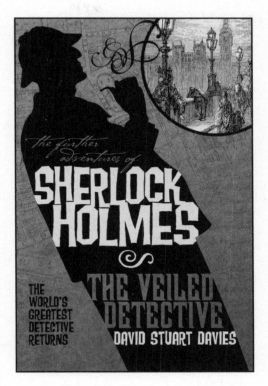

THE FURTHER ADVENTURES
OF SHERLOCK HOLMES

THE VEILED DETECTIVE

David Stuart Davies

It is 1880, and a young Sherlock Holmes arrives in London to pursue a
career as a private detective. He soon attracts the attention of criminal
mastermind Professor James Moriarty, who is driven by his desire to
control this fledgling genius. Enter Dr John H. Watson, soon to make
history as Holmes's famous companion.

ISBN: 9781848564909

AVAILABLE NOW!

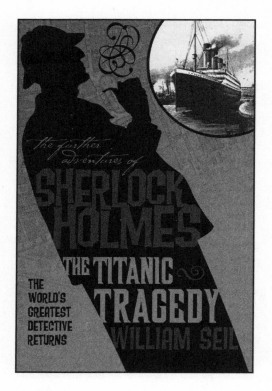

THE FURTHER ADVENTURES
OF SHERLOCK HOLMES

THE TITANIC TRAGEDY

William Seil

Holmes and Watson board the *Titanic* in 1912, where Holmes is to carry
out a secret government mission. Soon after departure, highly important
submarine plans for the US navy are stolen. Holmes and Watson work
through a list of suspects which includes Colonel James Moriarty, brother
to the late Professor Moriarty – will they find the culprit before tragedy
strikes?

ISBN: 9780857687104
AVAILABLE NOW!

THE FURTHER ADVENTURES
OF SHERLOCK HOLMES

THE WEB WEAVER

Sam Siciliano

A mysterious gypsy places a cruel curse on the guests at a ball. When
a series of terrible misfortunes affects those who attended, Mr Donald
Wheelwright engages Sherlock Holmes to find out what really happened
that night. Can he save Wheelwright and his beautiful wife Violet from
the devastating curse?

ISBN: 9780857686985

AVAILABLE NOW!

THE FURTHER ADVENTURES
OF SHERLOCK HOLMES

THE STAR OF INDIA

Carole Buggé

Holmes and Watson find themselves caught up in a complex chessboard
of a problem, involving a clandestine love affair and the disappearance
of a priceless sapphire. Professor James Moriarty is back to tease and
torment, leading the duo on a chase through the dark and dangerous
back streets of London and beyond.

ISBN: 9780857681218

AVAILABLE NOW!